# Inheritance of Night

William Styron

# Inheritance of Night

Early Drafts of *Lie Down in Darkness*

*With a preface by the author and an introduction*

*by James L. W. West III*

Duke University Press *Durham and London 1993*

Printed in the United States of America on acid-free paper ∞
Typeset in Berkeley Medium
Publication of this volume has been facilitated by the generosity
of The Friends of Duke University Library
The introduction to this volume appeared in an earlier form in the
French journal *Delta*, no. 23 (octobre 1986); portions are reprinted here
with permission. Styron's five-page prospectus for *Inheritance of Night* was
published in an appendix to the article.
Library of Congress Cataloging-in-Publication Data
Inheritance of Night : Early Drafts of Lie Down in Darkness /William Styron :
with a preface by the author and an introduction by James L. W. West III.
Includes bibliographical references.
ISBN 0-8223-1308-1 (lettered ed. : alk. paper).
ISBN 0-8223-1309-X (numbered ed. : alk. paper).
IBSN 0-8223-1310-3 (trade ed. : alk. paper)
1. Styron, William, 1925– —Manuscripts—Facsimiles. 2. Manuscripts,
American—Facsimiles. I. Title. PS3569.T9I54 1993
813'.54—dc20 92–26030 CIP

# Contents

# Preface

It's fascinating for me to read, for the first time in over forty years, the stumbling starts toward the creation of *Lie Down in Darkness*. These passages show how, in my early twenties, I may have been in possession of a luminous vision for a novel but how it was a luminosity clouded by much indecision and awkwardness. As my words now strike responsive chords of memory, I can see how well-prepared I was, emotionally, to set down my narrative but how ill-formed still was my sense of proportion and pacing, those elements of storytelling that elude so many beginning writers. Much of the present material was ultimately discarded from the ongoing manuscript of the book. Obviously I later found that these passages simply didn't correspond to my evolving needs. Some of the writing, however, remained almost word for word in the final version; the most notable example is the long description of the train ride from Richmond to "Port Warwick" which constitutes the novel's opening paragraphs.

I finished this beginning section a few months after I was fired from the McGraw-Hill Book Company, during the post-New Year's period of 1948, when I was living on upper Lexington Avenue in New York. All through a snowstorm—the worst in the northeast since the famous blizzard of 1888—I had been holed up in my chilly basement apartment reading Robert Penn Warren's *All the King's Men*. The beginning of that masterful novel also involves a trip, by car, and is told in the second person, evoking a vivid immediacy; still in thrall to Warren's book, I wrote about the train ride in an attempt to emulate the vigor of the original, and then went on to create the scenes of Milton Loftis and his companions waiting for the train at the Port Warwick station. Much later I substantially reworked the scenes which are published here, eliminating for instance the character of Marcus Bonner, who may have borne a pale resemblance to myself.

I also struck a bad snag in the writing process while I was living on Lexington Avenue. Somehow I felt that the book might proceed with greater ease if I moved away from the big city, which had begun to disenchant me for various reasons, not the least of which was a persistent financial ache. Since I had a number of friends in the Duke community, I decided to move back to Durham and try my luck there, where the winters were more tolerable, the rents reasonable, and the food, especially the delicious Carolina barbeque, within the scope of my dwindling resources. I then owned an extremely neurotic cocker spaniel named Mr. Chips, with whom I was emotionally entangled. Mr. Chips and I traveled south by train and took up residence in a new but nondescript apartment in a house on Fifth Street in West Durham.

One of my warmest welcomers was Professor William Blackburn, whose role as mentor while I was a student had been decisive in my seeking a career in writing, and who now made it clear that he was still ready to offer encouragement and, if need be, solace. The East Campus Library was close by, and I haunted its shelves. I had some good Duke friends, among them the late Ashbel Brice, editor of Duke Press, whose house nearby became a West Durham version of a literary salon, and Bob Loomis, who was then finishing his last year at the university and later became my editor at Random House. I also began a very satisfactory romantic arrangement with a fine-looking nurse at Duke hospital. Nurses, with their biological know-how, were esteemed for their atypical generosity in that erotic ice age. All should have been propitious for the creation of a first novel, but there were further snags.

Mr. Chips, for one thing, became *canis non grata* at my house, owned by an ill-tempered redneck who one day gave me seventy-two hours to get rid of my beloved friend or face eviction. I was distraught but so financially insecure that I couldn't move to another place, and was forced to convey ownership of the dog to a professor of philosophy on the Duke faculty. (I vowed to steel myself against the hurt by not seeing Mr. Chips again, fearful that my heart would break; when, two months later, I relaxed my resolve and paid him a visit he attacked me savagely.) More importantly, however, the book that was to become *Lie Down in Darkness* simply refused to stir, or be stirred, from its embryonic state and acquire the outlines and substance of a living, breathing novel.

It's clear that this had to do with a failure of conceptualization. By this I mean that I hadn't at that time worked out adequately in my mind an idea of the book's essential architecture, the invisible scaffolding so necessary to support the complex structure of character and event and dramatic revelation. The vision I possessed—and it was a passionate one, arousing me each day to what seemed prodigious efforts of concentration—was still in the realm of feeling; I hadn't found a way to subdue that feeling so that it would be obedient to the demands of narrative, blending with it to form the more or less symmetrically made, aesthetically satisfying object all novelists, young or old, yearn for their works to become. I was floundering, and remained floundering as I scribbled away on my yellow legal pads on the wobbly card table in the house on Fifth Street, often wondering if I shouldn't have gone into the foreign service, my first boyhood ambition. The handwritten notation I made on the final page of the present text doubtless sums up my mood at that time: *Or am I too far gone? Would like to write a war novel: these people give me the creeps.*

*Inheritance of Night,* then, is made up of the fragments of a beginning, bits of fruitful inspiration mingled with conceits that were stillborn. Most of it is the product of my frustrated but by no means worthless year in Durham. As I've said, certain portions are embedded verbatim, or nearly so, in the finally published work. So my time on Fifth Street could scarcely be regarded as a waste, no matter how indecisive the outcome of my labor. Still, I realized that again I had reached a dead end. And so once more I traveled back north to the metropolis, hoping that I might finally resolve the problems that had been driving me to distraction. Clearly I managed to do this, at least to my own satisfaction, in the two years that passed between the time I left Durham and the early spring day in 1951 when I wrote the last line of *Lie Down in Darkness.*

William Styron
Roxbury, Connecticut
April 5, 1992

# Introduction

Near the end of *Sophie's Choice*, William Styron's middle-aged narrator Stingo mentions the novel he was in the process of composing some thirty years earlier: "I had already fashioned for it an appropriately melancholy title: *Inheritance of Night*. This from the *Requiescat* of Matthew Arnold, an elegy for a woman's spirit, with its concluding line: 'Tonight it doth inherit the vasty hall of Death.'"[1] Most readers of *Sophie's Choice* know that the narrative is autobiographical, and some of them are probably able to identify broad parallels between the story and Styron's literary career. Few readers, however, would likely know that from 1947 to 1949 Styron did in fact work on a novel entitled *Inheritance of Night*, and that this novel was the unfinished predecessor of *Lie Down in Darkness* (1951). The original handwritten drafts of *Inheritance* no longer survive, but in March 1980 Styron's former literary agent Elizabeth McKee came upon the typescripts of *Inheritance* in her files and sent them to the novelist at his home in Roxbury, Connecticut. Styron forwarded these materials to the Manuscript Department of the William R. Perkins Library, Duke University, in March 1982. Today they are housed in the collection of his papers there.

These typescript materials—a prospectus, two lengthy beginnings, and a continuation of the second of these beginnings—are reproduced in this volume. They show young William Styron groping his way into his first novel, trying out various narrative strategies, and attempting with some success to discard the heavy influence of William Faulkner. These materials, studied in conjunction with Styron's extant letters from the late 1940s, reveal important information about the composition of *Lie Down in Darkness*. They also establish an unexpected link between Marcus Bonner, one of the characters in *Inheritance of Night*, and Stingo of *Sophie's Choice*.

In May 1947, Styron was living in New York City, working as an associate editor and manuscript reader for Whittlesey House, the trade-book division of

McGraw-Hill publishers. He was trying to begin a novel but was having little success, partly because the rooming house in which he was living was so dreary. "I find my present room on 11th street a completely depressing affair," he wrote to his father at about this time, "and I know I'd go mad if I had to stay pent up there for long."[2] By October 10, Styron had been fired from McGraw-Hill and had decided to work full-time on his novel. He had some savings in the bank and could draw twenty dollars a week from the Veterans Administration; later in October he learned that he and his father were to share a modest legacy. By having his father dole out the legacy to him in small monthly amounts, Styron was able to cover his expenses and work without distraction on his novel. He had moved to more suitable quarters on Lexington Avenue and had enrolled in editor Hiram Haydn's class in fiction-writing at the New School for Social Research. *Inheritance of Night* began to take shape, but progress was slow. A letter from Styron to his father, written on December 9, reveals hesitancy and self-doubt:

> I can't tell you how much this novel means to me. The process of sitting down and writing is pure torture to me, but at the same time I think about the book all the time and am in more or less a suspended state of worry and anxiety if I'm not writing. I worry, too, about the sincerity of my effort; if whether what I'm writing is not so much rhetoric, and it is only in my most now-self-critical mood that I can even come vaguely to realize that what I write does, in truth, have an element of truth in it and is, after all, a more faithful rendering of life than I believe it to be in my moments of doubt.

By early January, Haydn had persuaded Crown Publishers to give Styron a contract and an advance on his novel. The first fifty pages were nearing completion, and Styron was preparing a prospectus of the rest of the book. Portions of this initial draft were later reworked and published in *Lie Down in Darkness*, but Styron would have to rewrite the material extensively before he would be satisfied to publish it.

### *Prospectus and Typescript I*

The first version of *Inheritance of Night* is prefaced by epigraphs from Matthew Arnold and Euripides. In a note on the third leaf, Styron explains the narrative strategy: "I intend for this novel to be divided into three books of from ten to fifteen sections apiece. Each book is to be preceded by a monologue, direct or interior, which is intended to throw light upon Peyton and her story." The narrative begins with the first of the monologues, this one from Maudie Loftis, who has been placed in the Mordecai Clinic in Richmond by her father, Milton. But Maudie, in this monologue, is not the same character one finds in the published version of *Lie Down in Darkness*. In *Inheritance*, Maudie is only mildly retarded and speaks in an idiom that suggests lack of education rather than feeble-mindedness. Her monologue is delivered in September 1945, when she is almost thirty years old. She is angry over being institutionalized and believes that only an injured leg has held her back—that otherwise she is normal. Maudie ends her monologue: "I want to do things like other people and I think it's a shame that Papa put me in this place. I just want to be happy, I tell you."

Maudie's monologue is reminiscent of Benjy Compson's opening section in *The Sound and the Fury*. Though not nearly so backward mentally as Benjy, she has, like him, been brought up by an alcoholic father and a neurotic mother, and she has been sent to an institution, just as Benjy was sent to Jackson by Jason Compson. Styron was not satisfied with these pages, and he would drop them when he made a second attempt to begin his novel. He had not been able to suggest Maudie's retardation through her speech, and her section had sounded rather as if it were narrated by a backwoods countrywoman. In the published book Maudie is presented quite differently. She is so slow mentally that she is nearly mute, and she has become more symbol than character—an object for Helen's demented love and a representation of the emptiness of the Loftis marriage.

The second section of Typescript I is familiar to readers of *Lie Down in Darkness*. It is the initial passage of the published novel, the section that begins "Riding down to Port Warwick from Richmond. . . ." Styron patterned this section, with its direct address to the reader as "you," after the opening pages of Robert Penn Warren's *All the King's Men*.[3] This section was the only writing from *Inheritance of Night* with which Styron was truly pleased, and it remained essentially unchanged, except for a cut of nine lines, from Typescript I through all succeeding typescripts and into the published book.

The next twelve pages of Typescript I are similar to the corresponding section of *Lie Down in Darkness*. Here Styron presents the scene at the railroad station where

Peyton's body will shortly arrive, but in this early version only Milton Loftis, Ella Swan, and one undertaker meet the train. Riding in the train, however, and accompanying the body from New York, where he rescued it from a pauper's grave, is a character wholly absent from *Lie Down in Darkness*. His name is Marcus Bonner; he was a childhood classmate of Peyton's who, after college and service in the war, went to New York where he worked as a manuscript reader in a publishing house and "lived alone in a furnished room in a residence club." He has been infatuated with Peyton since childhood, but it was his older brother, Luther Bonner, who became one of Peyton's lovers. (Milton Loftis, partly out of revenge, has had an affair with Luther's wife Dolly.)[4] Originally Marcus must have been intended to play a central role in *Inheritance of Night*, but that role was reduced in the second version (Typescript II in the present volume). The character was dropped entirely from later versions and does not appear in *Lie Down in Darkness*.

Marcus is such a hesitant, Prufrockian character that *Lie Down in Darkness* is probably stronger without him. Styron, however, would carry the outlines of Marcus in his mind for the next twenty-five years, rethinking and reimagining him until he emerged as a quite different figure—Stingo, the narrator of *Sophie's Choice*. Stingo is similar to Marcus in many ways: both are young men with literary ambitions, both are manuscript readers, both live in dreary rooming houses, both are sensitive and observant, both are inclined to idealize women. But Stingo is feistier than Marcus, more confident and altogether more attractive. Part of the difference is in point-of-view: Stingo in *Sophie's Choice* is portrayed in the retrospective first-person mode by an older Stingo who views his younger self with humor and irony. In 1947 and 1948, Styron was not yet able to achieve this narrative detachment.

The next section of *Inheritance of Night* is told from Marcus's point-of-view. The most important revelation here comes as Marcus regards Milton Loftis and is "filled with an enormous contempt" when he remembers what Peyton had told him "one night in New York in a fury of grief and drunkenness." She had confessed "things he refused to believe until later when, carefully retrieving in his memory all those curious and unnamed gestures of the past, he came to know that the things she told him were true indeed." One suspects that Peyton had told Marcus of some kind of incestuous relationship between herself and her father—whether sexually consummated or not, one cannot tell from the surviving drafts. This incestuous element survives in *Lie Down in Darkness* though it is muted there, partly because of cuts in Peyton's final interior monologue that Styron's publisher, Bobbs-Merrill, insisted upon in 1951.[5]

The following section of Typescript I is narrated from the point-of-view of Mr. Casper, the undertaker; it appears on pages 18–23 of the published novel in considerably expanded form. Then we return, in the typescript, to Marcus's point-of-view: he remembers a school production of "Cinderella" in which Peyton played the title role and he was the page boy who tried the glass slipper on her foot. This material too would be dropped when Styron prepared the second typescript version.

The final portion of Typescript I is an early version of the first of the sections in *Lie Down in Darkness* that are narrated from Helen Loftis's point-of-view. Helen, in her bedroom, listens as the undertaker's limousine pulls away from her house; then she thinks about Milton, Maudie, and Peyton. Most of the scenes she recollects in the published book are present already in this early typescript, but they appear in *Lie Down in Darkness* in rewritten and expanded form, and in a different order.

Surviving with Typescript I is a five-page prospectus which Styron apparently prepared for Crown Publishers. Though the plot of *Inheritance* is markedly different from that of *Lie Down in Darkness*, the elements of the later novel are already present: alcoholism, adultery, failed love, suicide, the dissolution of an upper middle-class family, and the decadence of postwar southern society. In form this prospectus most nearly resembles the Compson Appendix to *The Sound and the Fury*, which Styron first encountered during the summer of 1947 in Malcolm Cowley's edition of *The Portable Faulkner*. He seems to have been trying here to imitate some of its features.[6]

In the prospectus and Typescript I, Styron's characters are beginning to come alive, but they appear not yet to have been fully conceived. Faulkner's influence is apparent, both in the prospectus and in much of the other writing. There are echoes of F. Scott Fitzgerald as well. The possible incest between father and daughter brings to mind *Tender Is the Night*, for example, and later, when Marcus recalls that Peyton's voice "had the sound of silver coins clinking together" one thinks of the famous description of Daisy Buchanan's voice in *The Great Gatsby*. Styron must have recognized that these influences were rather too apparent. He resolved to begin his novel over, cutting much material, expanding the salvaged sections, and attempting to forge his own distinctive prose style.

## *Typescript II*

First, however, Styron left New York and returned to live in Durham, on more familiar ground. By July 11, 1948, he was back in the city, temporarily staying with a friend; by July 21 he was installed in an apartment at 901 Fifth Street, near Duke's East Campus.[7] Early in September he contacted a literary agent for the first time; his choice was Elizabeth McKee, who had been recommended by a mutual friend at Whittlesey House. In his first letter to McKee, dated September 9, Styron mentions that he is writing a novel but admits that "only a small part" is finished. "I ain't no speedball," he notes. He is also working on several short stories, which he hopes McKee will be able to market for him. The novel, he thinks, will be finished "sometime in the middle of next year." Near the end of the letter he adds: "I'm twenty-three years old, and for some dreary and inexplicable reason I guess I'll keep at this writing business for a long time. Maybe it's because it's the only thing I know how to do with even a faint degree of competence."[8]

Styron settled in and began to rewrite the opening section of *Inheritance of Night*. By October 12, he had finished his revision and expansion and had sent a typescript of the material to McKee. In his covering letter, one can see that his conception of his novel had by this time crystallized into a form very close to the eventual pattern for *Lie Down in Darkness*:

> The story, in short, is nothing but that of a modern upper South middle-class family, and the daughter of the family, named Peyton Loftis. I've got no drum to beat, political or otherwise. I just want to give a picture of a way of life that I have known, and of the people therein. I probably have a moral purpose—the late Bliss Perry said that you *had* to have one—but it hasn't quite yet emerged. Anyway, Peyton, who is twenty-four and something of a bitch, has just died violently and I must say horribly in New York and is being returned to her home town for a hasty and unpublicized interment. What transpires on the one day of her burial is the burden of the novel. Gradually, through their memories, you get a picture of Peyton and, I hope, of the "way of life" of which I was speaking. If the story seems morbid it's because I'm probably morbid myself, although I've got some good ghastly humor later on.

This second typescript survives in two identical copies, a ribbon and a carbon, both among Styron's papers at Duke. It has no title page; letters from this period suggest that Styron had by now rejected *Inheritance of Night* as a title and was referring to his novel as *The Story of Peyton Loftis*. Typescript II begins with the epigraph from Euripides, then launches straight into the opening of the eventual published text: "Riding down to Port Warwick from Richmond. . . ." Maudie's monologue is gone, and the scene at the train station, which still follows the "Riding down" section, has been expanded. Now Milton and Dolly Bonner meet the train along with Ella Swan and two undertakers. Marcus Bonner is still on the train, but his role is diminished and he does not recall, in the limousine, any drunken revelations from Peyton. In this second typescript one finds the first mention of the radiator trouble that will delay the hearse in the published novel. In the earlier version Styron had slowed down the automobile by means of detours for Daddy Faith's followers and for road-repair gangs, but in Typescript II he used the more plausible device of radiator trouble on a hot August day.

Milton's recollections begin on page 9 of this second typescript: this time he is more obviously haunted by his father's disapproval of him and bothered by his memories of the old man's sententious advice. Beginning on page 18 one finds the eight-page section told from the undertaker's point-of-view. Marcus's recollections about grade school and the production of "Cinderella" are gone, though, and Helen's reverie in her bedroom has been considerably expanded and rewritten. The most noticeable change in Helen's section is the addition of her self-righteous satisfaction over Milton's grief. "*He is feeling it now*," she thinks. "*Perhaps now it will be upturned that chalice he has borne of whatever constant immeasurable selflove . . . upturned in this moment of his affliction and dishonor.*"

*Typescript III*

Styron continued to push ahead with his writing. In early January 1949, he visited New York and talked with Haydn and McKee, then returned to Durham and resumed work. By the first of March he had finished twenty more pages and had mailed them to Haydn. These pages also survive; they are reproduced as Typescript III in this volume. Some of this material would be included in the novel, but much of it would not. The first nine pages are similar to portions of *Lie Down in Darkness*: in this section Milton hears a lyric from a country song on a restaurant jukebox, then enters the restaurant where he becomes nauseated in the restroom. Next follows a five-page history of Port Warwick which traces the development of the city from a coaling stop to a shipbuilding center and explains the demographic origins of the population. The passages, though informative, are so transparently expository that they stand out awkwardly from the surrounding narrative. In the published book Styron would drop these pages and reveal information about Port Warwick in a different way, bit by bit through the recollections of his characters.

The final pages of Typescript III are a first attempt to develop the character of Dolly Bonner. She is a native of Port Warwick whose father died when she was fourteen, leaving her and her mother in straitened circumstances. Her mother had to take in boarders to make ends meet, and Dolly married one of them, "a fleshy, asthmatic man of about forty with soft hands and spectacles and a look of vague alarm." The boarder, named Albert Brokenborough, has a lung ailment and has come to Port Warwick for the sea air. He dies about a year after marrying Dolly, and she is left alone. Styron was displeased with this writing when he sent it to Haydn. At the bottom of the final page he noted: "Would like to write a war novel: these people give me the creeps."

Unhappy over the way his novel was going, Styron wrote a troubled letter to Haydn in mid-March. In his answering letter, Haydn suggested that it might be best for Styron to begin another manuscript. On April 15, Styron wrote Elizabeth McKee that he would move back to New York within two weeks. "Still under Mr. Haydn's guidance," he wrote, "I am beginning another novel—an elaboration of the prison story I told you about. The novel which I sent you just seemed to bog down. I had no idea where I was going. I'm sure the new novel will be better all the way around." This new project was to be a short narrative about Styron's experiences as a military prison guard on Hart's Island in New York Harbor during 1945.[9] This project too was stillborn, however, and Styron eventually returned to *Inheritance of Night* in the summer of 1949 after a brief residence in a rooming house at 1506 Caton Avenue in Brooklyn—the rooming house that became the model for Yetta Zimmerman's establishment in *Sophie's Choice*. Styron again rewrote the material he had shown Haydn and McKee (except for the "Riding down to Port Warwick" passage), and somehow, on this third attempt, the novel "took." Styron pushed ahead steadily through the rest of 1949 and all of 1950; in early April of 1951 he finished the manuscript of a novel he was now calling *Lie Down in Darkness*.

In reconstructing the history of *Inheritance of Night*, in ordering the typescripts and in studying the extant correspondence, one is struck by Styron's dogged persistence, his commitment to making himself into a good writer, and his refusal to let less than his best work pass. Probably he could have finished *Inheritance of Night* and published it, but it would not have been the novel that *Lie Down in Darkness* turned out to be. Styron had to wait for his own writing and thinking to mature. While waiting, he practiced by composing short stories and by manipulating the sections of narrative that he had already written, rather as one turns a kaleidoscope, searching for the position in which the colored fragments will combine to produce the most beautiful pattern. Only when he hit upon the proper arrangement was he able to proceed with the novel that would eventually establish his reputation.

## *Notes*

1. William Styron, *Sophie's Choice* (New York: Random House, 1979), p. 449.
2. Styron to W. C. Styron, Sr., dated "Saturday" in the former's hand and "May 1947" in the latter's. Styron's letters to his father are among the materials at Duke and are quoted here with his permission.
3. See Styron's memoir "Robert Penn Warren" in *This Quiet Dust and Other Writings* (New York: Random House, 1982), pp. 245–48.
4. None of these relationships is found in *Lie Down in Darkness*. Both Marcus and Luther are absent from the published book; Styron retains only the surname "Bonner" for Dolly and her husband Pookie.
5. Arthur D. Casciato, "His Editor's Hand: Hiram Haydn's Changes in Styron's *Lie Down in Darkness*," *Studies in Bibliography* 33 (1980), 263–76; reprinted in *Critical Essays on William Styron*, ed. Arthur D. Casciato and James L. W. West III (Boston: G. K. Hall, 1982), pp. 36–46.
6. Styron mentions *The Portable Faulkner* and comments on Cowley's influential introduction in a letter to his father dated 24 July 1947.
7. This apartment house still stands; Fifth Street has been renamed Sedgefield Street.
8. Styron's letters to Elizabeth McKee are among the Harold Matson Papers at the Butler Library, Columbia University; they are quoted here with permission.
9. No drafts of this early attempt to fictionalize the Hart's Island experience survive, but in the summer of 1953, while living in Italy, Styron again tried without success to write a novella based on his stint as a prison guard. The seven-thousand-word aborted opening is among his papers at the Library of Congress; it was published as "Blankenship" in *Papers on Language and Literature*, special Styron issue, 23 (Fall 1987), 430–48.

# PROSPECTUS

*(Winter 1947-48)*

"Inheritance of Night"

THE STORY OF PEYTON LOFTIS

This novel beats no drum, makes no moral, rights no wrong. It is a picture of part of life as I have seen it and of the lives of people I have known - although of the lives of various and dissimilar people, none of whom could be identified singly with any of the characters in this book. Mainly it is the story of a girl who although not the typical American girl shares at least part of the nature of her contemporaries in that her life, while perhaps no more happy a life had it been lived in another age, might in some measure appeared then a bit less futile. She was bound in a web of glittering days and dark, fury-driven nights and although she would have been the last person to use the word "lonely" in regard to herself, she died as she lived, in loneliness. This is the story of:

PEYTON LOFTIS. Born in 1922 of patrician parents in the seacoast city of Port Warwick, Virginia, she died at the age of twenty-four, in 1946, in New York, lying for twelve days and nights - silent at last, decapitated, and calcimine white - on a stretcher in the city mortuary on East Twenty-ninth Street, after which, when the legal time was concluded, she was hauled away in a pine box along with twenty-six others in a rattling green truck to the paupers' cemetery. When she was disinterred some weeks later, upon the intervention of a young man whom she had never loved, it was found that the flesh - upon which so many lovers (in her last days lovers of all ages, sizes, colors, and degrees of intoxication) had tendered caresses in every conceivable variation of passion, wonder, gentleness, and lust — that this self-same flesh, which Peyton herself had stroked so admiringly and tenderly after each fragrant bath, had reached such a state of putrefaction in Potter's Field (it was August) that the authorities, even more annoyed than the three prisoners assigned to transfer the remains into the chromium interior of a Chambers' hearse, considered for a moment the advisability of leaving the body there to resume its process of gradual, anonymous decay. Upon the urgent demands, however, of the young man whom she had never loved, what was left of Peyton was placed in a Health Department-inspected, hermetically sealed case and loaded aboard a baggage car in Pennsylvania Station and was eventually delivered to Port Warwick, although some four hours late, since the train itself was derailed near Fredericksburg, Virginia, partially wrecking the baggage car and slightly damaging the case. At the private burial the next day at the Warwick Memorial Park were the following spectators and mourners:

MILTON LOFTIS, age fifty-four, father of Peyton, portly, handsome, his face slightly flushed with sunburn and the prolonged effects of bonded Bourbon whiskey, which he loved dearly. He was aware then for the first time, as he gazed at the cool pine grove beyond Route 60, not so much of the tragedy of life, in his own particular case, but merely of its swift passing. He was married to an influentual and wealthy woman and it was only rarely, although intensely, that he experienced a painful sense of guilt when he realized that it was through her alone that he had conducted such a successful and lucrative practice of law. In only two apparent ways did he differ from his colleagues. One was that, unlike them, his affair with another woman occurred only once and then at an age when one would think that abstinence for so many years might have indicated moral compunction, or at least a dogged lack of interest. Especially in the light of his almost slavish devotion to his younger daughter, Peyton, a love so devouring, an attachment so intense that it in itself comprised the other manner - at least the outward manner - in which he seemed different from the others.

HELEN LOFTIS, age forty-nine, mother of Peyton, wife of Milton. Born Helen Peyton in Fort Sheridan, Illinois, the daughter of an independently wealthy Army colonel, she spent her early life in peacetime Army camps and boarding schools but nevertheless developed into an intelligent woman with sanguine ambitions for her husband, a fastidious housekeeper, and an impeccable hostess of notable charm. When, in the year following the second World War, her husband left her for Dolly Bonner and her elder daughter, Maudie - a retarded girl of twenty-nine - killed herself after a thwarted love-affair with a taxi-driver, she herself attempted self-destruction by poison, was saved by a stomach pump, and, after promising the Episcopal rector, Mr. Carr, "never to do it again," she disappeared into the big house on the Boulevard and was seen only once in a while - a stooped, white-haired old woman who took walks in the garden and could be seen from the Boulevard, upon occasion, standing beneath a sycamore, jerking her hands spasmodically toward the sun.

MARCUS BONNER, age twenty-seven. Born in Port Warwick. The young man whom Peyton never loved. He spent his adolescence in indolent and harmless pursuits, paid helpless court to Peyton's attentions, and watched in agony as she accepted and vanquished one after another of his companions. After college and the experience of war dimmed his memory of her he went to New York where he was employed by a book publisher to read and pass judgment on manuscripts with such titles as: "Tall Grows the Eelgrass" and "World Peace: A Solution." He lived alone in a furnished room in a residence club, the only young person in a palace of crushed hopes and lingering memories. He met Peyton long after her affair with his brother, Luther, although not so long after her brief marriage to Sidney Harris. And loving her once more, and loathing her, he watched her as she neared the end of that road which she set out on fifteen years before, that day when, as a child scolded by her mother for wearing lipstick, she retorted: "I know what I'm doing."

SIDNEY HARRIS, age twenty-six. Born in New York City. He fell in love with Peyton when she came to New York to art school. He was caught by the same beauty that had held all the others. She thought him intellectual and profound. The marriage, which lasted seven months, was consecrated at the Loftises' home by the Reverend Mr. Carr, following which no announcement was made of the affair, and Mrs. Loftis went to bed for two days because Peyton was already pregnant (everybody knew that), and furthermore Sidney was a Jew. In New York again, a few weeks after the baby was born, Peyton, who despized everything she needed the most to love, tried to drown the infant in a bathtub, and would have succeeded had not Sidney broken the door down and taken the child from her. The same day he left without saying a word and she never saw him or her baby again, and didn't care.

The following were not present at the burial. Some were thinking of Peyton, however, and some were dead:

LUTHER AND DOLLY BONNER. Marcus's elder brother and his wife. It was Dolly who wrote the society column for the local morning newspaper and who at the Huntington Country Club one night made Milton Loftis tell her, in a buoyant spasm of too-much-whiskey and laughter how much he loved her - words that he remembered with a sudden shock the following morning when he realized that after all these years he did love her, indeed. And Peyton, half in revenge, half in despair because her father no longer loved her in the same way, took up with Dolly's husband, Luther, who was a draughtsman in the shipyard and sang tenor in the choir of St. Mark's Episcopal Church.

MAUD LOFTIS. Born in Port Warwick. In her the same madness that Milton Loftis had fathered in his younger daughter worked a gentler, but just as fatal necessity. When she died, by throwing herself off the seawall, she was nearly thirty years old, with the mind of a child of twelve. A gaunt, masculine face and an accident as a child, which cost her a leg, made her the victim all her life of Peyton's fury. Although she had two lovers in her life - one a gardener, the other a taxi-driver, she found no love at all. Her life was spent in hoping, and dying for her, finally, was no more terrible than going to sleep.

HUGH BONNER, age sixty-two. Born in Plymouth, North Carolina. Spent his days at sea. Pride, and not women, ruined him. Upon the death of his divorced wife he left his two sons, Marcus and Luther, in the care of his married sister in Port Warwick. He knew very little of either of his sons when, dying of cancer in the Norfolk Marine Hospital, Luther and Peyton paid him a visit and persuaded him to sign over his will from Marcus's to Luther's name. The next day he died, not thinking of his sons at all, but dreaming of a life raft and a horrible cabin boy in the middle of the Indian Ocean, and something soft and unutterably kind named Irma, in Bremerhaven, long ago.

Also present at the burial but off to the side a little, beneath the poplar tree, because she was a Negro, was:

ELLA SWAN, the Loftises' cook, age seventy-one, born in Port Warwick. She was the only friend, besides her father, that Peyton ever had. God to her was Father Charity who drove down from Baltimore every August in a glittering Cadillac to baptize the faithful in Hampton Roads. She alone understood.

# TYPESCRIPT I

*First Beginning (Winter 1947-48)*

Hold

I N H E R I T A N C E  O F  N I G H T

by

William Styron

Strew on her roses, roses,
   And never a spray of yew!

Matthew Arnold

My life hath known no father,
   Any road to any end may run . . .

<u>Iphigenia in Tauris</u>

[I intend for this novel to be divided into three books of from ten to fifteen sections apiece. Each book is to be preceded by a monologue, direct or interior, which is intended to throw light upon Peyton and her story.]

B O O K  O N E

A Vision of Death in August

MAUDIE LOFTIS, at the Mordecai Clinic, Richmond, Virginia, September, 1945.

[ital.]

LORD, I don't know how many times I remember seeing Papa come tearing up the lawn when I'd be sitting there sewing on the porch. I sewed a lot that summer. A sampler I remember I did for old lady Dyke who was in the hospital. She died before I was finished but I remember how much trouble it took because Mama taught me a lot of new things about sewing - stitching she called it - and I did that sampler in blue and red with a verse on it that went *God bless our home a happy one.* I forget the rest but Peyton would laugh at me every afternoon and say that it was old-fashioned and I could hear Mama holler out, "Hush, Peyton, hush." Peyton was around nine years old then, I recken, because she's six years younger than me and I was fifteen then. Fifteen then because that's how old I was when I got out of The School. And it was that summer that I sat on the porch every afternoon and worked on the sampler. They taught me at The School. And I'd sit there in the swing out of the sun, moving every once in a while when the sunshine would hit me, you know, and then Papa would come home, tearing up the lawn yelling "Peyton, Peyton!" I couldn't see him for the hydrangeas but I could hear his voice. Lord, that was a long time ago, but I remember it plain. I was fifteen then because I remember Peyton had her ninth birthday then.

She was born in June and she's six years younger than me. "Peyton, Peyton," I could hear Papa holler, and the dog - his name was Dover. He's dead now but his name was Dover because that's what Peyton called him when she was a baby and couldn't say the name right. I think his name was really Rover or something - he'd run out barking at Papa and Papa would come up the steps with sweat on his face and pat me on the back and say "Hello, Maudie, honey," and run right into the house hollering, "Peyton, Peyton." And Peyton would be hid somewhere in the house and he'd rush all over inside, I could hear him inside whistling and then she'd come out from wherever she was hid and if they were near the window I could see him pick her up and kiss her, him laughing and her laughing just like that. Oh I reckon she was his favorite, all right. He'd call her his little glamor girl and then Mama would holler out from the sunporch in the back. I could hear her say, "Milton, Milton, please try to be quiet, my migraine is so bad today," and they'd hush up, Papa and Peyton, and then they'd come out of the house real quiet, whispering together like he wasn't any older than her, and go up to Powhatan Road and get some ice-cream and bring me back some..Lord, it was hot that summer. I couldn't walk very far, just like now, on account of my leg, and while they'd be gone I'd sit there and sew and watch the water. We live on the water, on Hampton Roads. Papa always said it was the best place for a house in Port Warwick, where we live, and I guess so. In the summer the water is real blue and you can see the battleships and airplane carrirs and all. When Peyton got older Papa would take her out clamming and Mama and me would sit on the porch and drink ice tea and watch them way out in the low tide looking like sticks, Papa teaching Peyton how to clam. I couldn't ever go on account of my leg, you know, and I never wanted to go much anyhow because, Lord, I always thought clams and oysters are the messiest things there are. I like fish and softshell crabs and all, but clams and oysters are messy. Mama didn't ever go with them clamming. She didn't think it was dignified. That's what she'd say. "Milton, why don't you let Clay get those clams? I think it looks awful undignified for you to do that." And Papa would say, "Where's all your spirit, Helen?" That's what he'd say. Clay's our nigger boy, only he's not with us any more. He left a long time ago. Papa said he went up North where he could make more money. I don't know. But Papa would always take Peyton clamming. We live on the Boulevard and there are a lot of houses around us but we own the beach and we had a boat, too, until the storm blew it away. We own the clams, too. Papa was always down there on the beach with Peyton in the summer, building sand houses and all. That is, when he wasn't playing golf. He used to love golf. He doesn't play any more because he's got heart trouble, I think. He's a lawyer and he played golf with all of his and Mama's friends. They were mostly doctors and lawyers that belonged to the country club because they were the only ones in Port Warwick that had any money, Papa always said. But some of the bosses in the shipyard used to play, too. Me and Mama would sit there watching Papa and Peyton way out clamming, watching them go down the beach until they weren't any bigger than sticks, the sunlight shining down and the water real green, until you couldn't see them any more and all you could see was the beach stretching down in a kind of curve to Old Point and Norfolk across the water looking real little with the smoke coming up and making the sky smoky and all. Mama would sit there on the swing by me until you couldn't see them any more, looking mad and saying that Papa forgot all about her when Peyton was around. And then she'd go in and tell Ella Swan - she's our nigger cook - to cook dinner and she'd come out and stroke my hair and say, "my dear little darkeyed girl," and then she'd go back on the sunporch and lie down. I'd just sit there and sew on that old sampler until Papa and Peyton would come back around six o'clock with mud all over their legs and they'd be laughing together like they always did. Peyton was only nine years old but she was smart, Lord, she was smart, like she is now I reckon, and Papa and her would be talking together like she wasn't any younger than him at all. Once Peyton put a clam down my neck and Lord didn't I scream. I just hollered and cried and Mama came out and slapped Peyton good and hard. "Didn't I tell you to quit teasing her?" Mama said, and Peyton cried and Mama cried and I was crying fit to kill. Papa came out and told Mama to quit slapping Peyton and they argued something awful and I walked out on the breakwater and watched the ships. Lord, I remember that summer so well. Papa and Peyton never went clamming together any years after that because I guess Peyton was growing up and she had a lot of friends in school and all. I never went to public school myself, on account of my leg. I mean I was in public school for a while in the first and second grades but I never could do my work as good as the other children on account of my leg and finally Mama and Papa took me out and sent me to a private teacher named Miss Barton. I don't remember much about her. Then when I got a little older they sent me to The School up in Maryland. I was up there five years. It was built like a home, almost, and there were fifteen girls besides me. It was on a green hill looking down on a river and an old woman named Mrs. Flame was the principal. Lord, she was mean. She used to call us "miss." <u>Miss</u> Loftis this and <u>Miss</u> Loftis that until I thought I would go crazy. I was always crying that first year, I was so homesick. One time Mrs. Flame called me into her office and told me I was a silly little ninny and I went out crying and tripped on the floor getting out of there - Lord, I had such a time with my leg until I got grown up - and she tried to help me up, saying, "I'm sorry, dear girl," and I hit her with my hand and got up and went up to my room and put all my stuff in a bag and was going home. I would have gone, too, but Mrs. Flame came up and said she was sorry and not to go home. She sure acted worried. Well, I didn't go home but I stayed in my room and cried for a long time until Miss Monahan came up and told me not to grieve. Oh, she was wonderful. I'll always remember that Miss Monahan. She was so pretty. Always wanting to help you and all, and calling you Maudie instead of miss. She taught arithmetic and horseback riding. I could ride, too, even with my leg, and Miss Monahan was always saying with that smile of her's, "You'll be the best of them all." And I was pretty good, too. When I started bleeding the first time I was so scared I wanted to die. I hid in the closet and stuffed handkerchiefs in my mouth to keep from screaming, I wanted to scream so bad. I passed out in arithmetic class that morning and the niggers took me up to my room and Mrs. Flame was going to call the doctor but Miss Monahan said, no, she knew what was wrong and she told them all to go away and she sat down and told me in that soft voice of her's what was wrong, you know, how girls get that sort of thing and all, and how I was more worried than sick. I could have kissed her then. I guess I loved her more than anybody except Harvey, and now Harvey's gone. I wrote love letters to her a long time, even after I got out of school but finally I just sort of stopped. She wrote me that she was going to get married and move to California and I was awful jealous for a while, but that was years ago and I've almost forgotten what she looks like. When I came back to Port Warwick from The School everything was real strange for a while but I finally got used to being at home and helping Mama around the house, just like I got used to The School and even Mrs. Flame after I was there for a while. I made good grades there and I pestered Mama all summer after I got out of The School about going to prep school. I wanted to go to St. Mary's, that's the school that all the girls from our church in Port Warwick go to and Mama said she'd think about it, but I never did go to any prep school or college or anything after The School. One time I got in a fight with Peyton that summer, I forget what over, but Peyton kicked me in my leg, you know, this one, and called me crazy and feeble-minde and all until I got up and threw a book at her. I cried, too, and Mama came out and made Peyton say she was sorry. We never did have any fights after that and Peyton said she didn't mean to say it. Sometimes when I remember what she said I get to thinking that Mama and Papa didn't send me to St. Mary's because I was dumb. But I know that's not so because Dr. Meekins - he's the doctor up here, you know, that I've been coming to ever since my accident when I was a baby - he said that I was as smart as anybody my age, except that my leg has kept me back, that's all. And it's true. I am as smart as Peyton, or anybody. Even if Peyton did go to St. Mary's. Even if she can paint pictures and all. Sometimes I want to hate Peyton because she's so smart and beautiful. I've had a man to love me, too, and I think it's a shame just because Harvey's a gardener Mama and Papa called the police and carried me up to this old hospital again. Lord, I hate it. I hate every bit of it. I'm just as good as anybody. Haven't I got a right to love somebody, just as much as anybody else? I know about Peyton and I know about Papa, too. Peyton loving Luther

Bonner and Papa loving Luther's wife. I know all about it. And I think it's a shame that Mama has to stay alone at home, trying to be happy about everything. Luther Bonner is better than his wife and I don't much blame Peyton if she wants to. But Papa ought to be ashamed. And putting me in this hospital just because I love Harvey. He was so good to me. What if he is married? He loved me, he told me so, and I don't care if he is almost as old as Papa. Yes he loved me, I know it. We were in the garden behind the trellis and he kissed me and called me his blackeyed Susan and he felt me all over and he said he wanted me. And I let him do it to me, right there. It was the first time and I could smell the ferns and the azaleas somewhere. And it wasn't like what Peyton said it was like but it was wonderful all the same feeling his body up next to me and feeling his heart beating and hearing him say "oh, honey" over and over again. But he wanted me, he wanted to take me away, he said. That was the best. And what good is it for me to be in this place here when I have a memory like that, just as happy and natural memory as anybody else? I'm almost thirty years old now and I have a right to be happy just like anybody. Sometimes I stay awake at night and remember the thoughts I had when I was already grown and Peyton had started going with Eddie Boutchard and I could see them parked in the car at night and I knew what they were doing. And I'd go back to bed and listen to the silence in the house and look out across the water and see the lights blink on and off at the naval base. I'd throw off the sheets it would be so hot, and I'd listen again and hear the baby squalling in the house next door, sounding far-off and faint, like the noise you hear in a dream. Then there would be footsteps on the sidewalk and the hot summer night outside and Peyton's voice, low like it always was, "Goodnight, Eddie . . .goodnight . . .

goodnight . . . goodnight," and silence again. I'd get to wanting something terrible, way inside, down here, almost like a pain. And I'd turn my head so I could feel the breeze from the water touch my face and the wanting would get so bad that I could have hollered out anything, "Take me!" or "My darling!" or anything. Anything, I tell you, to take away the pain. Then I'd go to sleep and in the morning I'd open my eyes and the sun would be shining down on my face. That's the way it is now sometimes. I want to get out of here. I want to be happy like other people. I want to do things like other people and I think it's a shame that Papa put me in this place. I just want to be happy, I tell you.

I

RIDING down to Port Warwick from Richmond the train begins to pick up speed on the outskirts of the city, past the tobacco factories with their ever-present, hovering haze of faintly acrid dust and past the rows of uniformly-brown, clapboard houses which stretch down the hilly streets for miles, it seems, the hundreds of rooftops all reflecting the pale light of dawn; past the suburban roads still sluggish and sleepy with early-morning traffic, and rattling swiftly now over the long bridge which separates the last two hills where in the valley below you can see the James River winding beneath its acid-green, malignant crust of scum out past the chemical plants and more rows of uniformly-brown, clapboard houses and into the woods beyond. Suddenly the train is burrowing through the pine woods and the conductor, who looks middle-aged and respectable, like someone's favorite uncle, lurches through the car asking for tickets. If you are particularly alert at that unconscionable hour you notice his voice, which is somewhat guttural and negroid - certainly vaguely fatuous-sounding after the accents of New York or Columbus or wherever you came from -, and when you ask him how far it is to Port Warwick and he says, "aboot eighty miles," you know you're in tidewater Virginia.

Then you settle back in your seat, your face feeling unwashed and swollen from the intermittent sleep you got sitting up the night before, and your gums sore from too many cigarettes, and you try to doze off, but the nap of the blue felt seat prickles your neck and so you sit up once more and cross your legs, gazing drowsily at the pipe manufacturer from Allentown, P-A, next to you, who told you last night about his hobby, model trains, and the joke about the two college girls at the Hotel Astor, and whose sleek white face, sprouting a faint gray crop of fine stubble, one day old, is now peacefully relaxed and immobile in sleep, his breath issuing from slightly parted lips in delicate sighs. Or, turning away, you look out at the pine woods driving past at sixty miles per hour, the trees standing close together, green and somnolent, and the brown-needled carpet of the forest floor dappled brightly in the early morning light, until the white fog of smoke from the engine ahead swirls and dips against the window like a tattered scarf, and obscures the view.

Later the woods thin out into fields green and nodding with rows of corn, the corn getting brown because it's August, and later still as the train dips into the tidelands the fields merge into acres of wooded bottoms where the pines grow tall, standing in marshes deep in saw-grass and murky with the brackish ooze that seeps off the river. Here the horse-doctors flit soundlessly with small, swift flutterings of irridescent wings, searching for grubs in the algae-green water, and at night, standing on the highway, you can hear a hound baying through the darkness. Now the sun is up and you see the mist lifting off the fields and in the middle of the fields the solitary cabins with their slim threads of smoke trailing out of plastered chimneys and the glow of a fire through an open door and then, at a crossing, the sudden, swift tableau of a Negro and his hay-wagon, and a lop-eared mule: the Negro with his mouth agape, exposing calcimine teeth, staring in astonishment at the speeding train, until the smoke obscures him, too, from view, and the one dark brown hand held cataleptic in the air.

Stirring, the pipe manufacturer squints sleepyeyed out at the sunlight and grunts, "Where are we?" and you murmur "Not far from Port Warwick, I hope," and as he turns on his side to sleep some more you finger your copy of the Richmond Times-Dispatch which the newsboy sold you an hour ago, and which you haven't read and won't read because maybe you have things on your mind; and instead you look out once more at the late summer landscape and the low, sorrowful beauty of the tide-land swamps and the pine-shadowed creeks - turgid, involute, and secret - winding through marshes full of small, darting, frightened noises and glistening and dead silent at noon except for a whistle, far off, and a distant rumble on the rails. Then the fields once more, and the shacks, and now and then a white-painted house where you can see a truck standing in the yard and a sycamore which casts a trembling light on the ground and a farmer, one overalled leg on the running board, about to climb in the truck, but with his head turned toward the train, staring. Then the house is gone and the sycamore with its tender, trembling light, and the fields again, hot and dusty and sending up greasy waves of heat, and the marshland again. And you think about the farmer for a moment, wondering where he's going and what his wife looks like - but you forget him, because you see a sign on the bordering highway which points to Port Warwick and that, most likely, is where you're going.

Port Warwick is a shipbuilding city and the workers' houses begin where the marshlands end - the clean, cheap clusters of plywood cottages springing out of the woods like toadstools - and now the men are going to work, their automobiles creeping southward along the highway past more groups of houses encroaching suddenly upon the desolation of the marshlands, the houses themselves backed up against the forest wall where, in their tiny back yards, the women are hanging clothes in the morning sunlight, turning pale white faces slowly toward the train going by. The train slows down and the pipe manufacturer wakes, perplexed and sleepy, and borrows your newspaper and drowsily studies the market reports and when you turn again the wilderness is gone, the suburban houses are rolling by, and the gray, anonymous streets, and the Super Market signs. Then the town itself, which from the train looks like any other small city since one side of the tracks - in this case the Negro section - presents a less imposing view than the other side, which belongs to the white people; and then the freight yards - you are going slowly now beneath the overpasses - and finally the halt at the station which is the end of the line because beyond the station is the river which is five miles wide and a deep salty green.

You get up and say goodbye to the pipe manufacturer, who is going on to Norfolk by ferry, and you get your bag off the rack and climb down off the train onto the station dock where the smell of the water is clean and refreshing after the flatulent warmth of the car and where, thirty yards away, your girl or your friends are waiting with expectant grins. "Oh, there he is!" and as you walk toward them you've already forgotten the pipe manufacturer forever, and the ride down. It's going to be a hot day.

On a weekday morning in late August in 1946 four people were assembled on the railroad dock at Port Warwick. The four, who stood closely together - three white men and a Negro woman past seventy -

On a weekday morning in late August in 1946 four people were assembled on the railroad dock at Port Warwick. The three, who stood closely together - two white men and a negro woman past seventy - could hardly have been distinguishable from the dozen or so other people awaiting the train were it not for two things which, to a more than casual observer, set them immediately apart. One was the fact that it might appear curious that twoose such affluent-looking men - certainly they were "gentlemen" - so obviously dressed for an occasion, were to be seen at such an inauspicious hour (it was fifteen minutes past nine by the station clock) in the company of a solitary and aged Negro woman who, in turn, was dressed in clothes worn only on Sunday and to funerals. The other was the fact that the face of one of the men wore a look of profound and troubled agitation. The other man, younger than his companion and dressed in black, his hands encased in gloves the color of house mice, seemed nonetheless to convey an air of sympathetic and thoughtful awareness, but for the most part he remained silent.

The sky was clear and cloudless and a deep violent blue, the sort of morning that promises heat and vague, langorous activity all day long. The air, already humid, smelled of creesete and tar and the dead fish which had been basking in the sunlight on the end of the dock for three or four days. Across from the dock and separated from it by fifty yards of slick greasy water a freighter lay tethered to its pier. Into its hold a gang of stevedores had begun to load a cargo of bauxite. From the pier there came the clanking metallic rattle of an electric crane and a workman's voice from the hold, sounding like the echo from a cave, "Come up there      come up there!" Drifting up from the hold a dense fog of dust had begun to shimmer brick red in the sunlight and floated like smoke in a dense, undulating, ruddy cloud, settling gently on the dock and covering everything with a fine dusty sediment the color of rust. Most of the waiting people on the dock retreated into the station, pounding their clothes with their hands, but the two men and the Negro woman waited patiently beside the tracks while the haze settled upon them silently, seeping into their clothes and encrusting the wrinkled face of the old woman in a dusty mask.

They stood for a while in the sunlight, none of them apparently noticing the dust sifting down except the younger man who at intervals tapped delicately at his gloves and who furtively withdrew a gold pocket-watch from his black-vested paunch, inspected it quickly, and then gazed hopefully up the tracks. And with a sudden abashed look he turned away, regarding with studied and gentle commiseration the other man, who remained silent out of some compulsion he could not explain even to himself - *because God knows, he thought, I need someone to talk to* - and who gazed out at the river now through the dust, at the green tidal water glistening with dancing blades of light. He was in his middle fifties and had been good-looking in his youth (one could see that); though traces of handsomeness remained his face had fallen into negligent disrepair - a young man's face thickly distended into an unhealthy flabbiness, the skin over well-formed bones now porous and deeply flushed. Through his sparse brown hair ran a wide streak of steel gray which had been there ever since adolescence and which, far from being disfiguring, had provided an added flourish to his appearance, a focal point toward which strangers might direct admiring looks; about this streak of gray he had been quite vain, and because of it he rarely wore a hat.

I shall not think too much about this thing, he thought, I shall try to occupy my mind with the water instead, knowing somehow as he thought that he could not circumvent immediacy by thinking of the future (when he was a young man his moments of gloom bacame more bearable by merely saying to himself: Soon all of this will be over, perhaps tomorrow I shall be drunk and happy and possibly I'll even have a woman) because now the future was more dismal to contemplate than the present. So because what he had to face in the immediate future (the reason he was on the dock) was bad enough and the time beyond that would be, inevitably, even worse, he confined his thoughts to the water and in the distance the forested ridge of deep blue which was the other shore. Perhaps, he thought, if I think only of this second this moment the train wont come at all perhaps its possible to make time stop by not acknowledging the future

by merely thinking of realizing that he was too old now and too weary for paradoxes, that the train would come after all, bringing with it the final, positive proof of fate and circumstance which all his life he had passively denied, believing (he an Episcopalian) or rather faintly understanding that the word Fate was merely one of those words like Conscience or Will which festooned the structure of the liturgy like pale plaster gargoyles and which became an imminent meaningful thing only in the Greek plays he had read in college years ago, and then in a cloudy and abstract manner; bringing with it (he saw, his mind advancing hesitantly into that future he could not accept, the train squeaking and shuddering to a stop, ponderous on the dock as it would appear five minutes hence or ten, the white steam panting upward and mingling with the drifting asthmatic fog of dust) the conclusive totality of all his errors and yet all his love (because he loved his daughter more than anything) and his life indeed, which was begun fifty-four years ago in a cluttered museum of a house in Washington, DC, where his first memory was a sunny room murmurous with the sad hushed sounds of Sunday afternoon and a parade outside on the street with distant band music both bright and disconsolate and his mother's voice whispering *Its President Cleveland going by, Milton dear Listen dear.* And again, his mind wandering compulsively into that minuscule portion of the future which separated the Now and the arrival of the train on the dock - *the train now is on the outskirts of town, he thought, and passing with a terrible rumbling noise over the last creek and the nigger shacks on the banks* - he knew, with a sudden luminous intensity, less a thought than a sound in his head, that it was all too dreadful for him to have to bear.

•

"Ella" "Ella, what am I going to do?"

The Negro woman turned her face toward him. The dust had inflamed the wrinkled old skin in a blaze of orange. Peering out of cave-like sockets, her eyes blinked moistly. "Now you just set tight, Cap'n Loftis," she said. "Me and Mr. Casper'll take care of things nice and easy. You just set tight." The man behind them made a quick noiseless motion with his lips - at once hesitant and a bit sorrowful - but no sound came forth; he remained silent and looked up the tracks. "You just trust in the Lord," Ella said.

In five minutes by the station clock - the flyspecked white disk, reading Bulova, emitted a faintly audible whirr above them - the train would arrive. Beyond the dock white sparks of sunlight twinkled on the water. On the freighter a brick-red figure scurried along a catwalk and stopped and peered into the hold. From the depths the hollow voice echoed, "Come up there!" In five minutes - above, the attenuated grimy finger of the minute hand jerked ahead with a clicketing sound - *no, four now, he thought* - the train would arrive, its arrival substantially meaningful in that it would signify his own departure just as (the lawyer in him speaking now) the pronouncement of guilty by a jury foreman generally assures an immediate and thorough dispatch and so in its coming would in a way symbolize the complete and irrevocable consummation of his minutes, hours, years, not only the hushed, murmurous hours which he remembered as a baby - the sunlight seeping in through gently rustling blinds and he, lying on something soft, watching the afternoon shadows bloom around him and his mother's hovering face, long forgotten now because she died before he could picture in his consciousness those features his father later said were refined and lovely - but beyond that the days of his childhood, of which he remembered walks in Rock Creek park with his father and the damp ferny smell of the woods and his best friend, a boy named Charley Quinn, who had a pale face and cheeks with famished hollows and a birthmark on his cheek like a brown-petalled flower, and who was killed at the Somme. And his father, who was a lawyer, descended from a long line of lawyers - until his death in 1920 he sported stiff wing collars and a twitching Edwardian moustache - had neither the prescience to avoid pampering his son nor to realize that sending him to the University of Virginia to study law, unprepared and at the age of seventeen, would produce the results it did: at nineteen he was a campus character known as "Blow," a drunkard even by fraternity standards, who drank because, fatherless, he found the sudden freedom oppressive and because, too, he liked the taste of whiskey and its attendant effect, in his case, of surpassing goodwill. Because he combined glibness with a natural curiosity he was moderately successful as a student and when, in his twentyfourth year, he was graduated from the law school, he was pleasantly surprised upon reviewing his record that he had performed so well, considering the fact that he had spent a preposterous amount of time drunk and in the town whorehouse, run by an elegant mulatto named Carmen Metz. And when the war broke out, although he did not shirk duty exactly (for two months he made gestures toward joining the Army which years later he still had to confess to himself were trifling and excursive), he was greatly relieved when his father procured for him, through government connections, a commission in the Army legal branch and he was sent to Governor's Island in New York City where, by processes infinitely more simple than he had ever imagined they would be, he was promoted in quick succession to first lieutenant and then to captain (a title which he retained throughout his civilian life), emerging from the war with that rank, and with the colonel's daughter. They met at an officers' dance on the island; her name was Helen Peyton. That night they walked along the seawall together in a drizzling rain and when he bent over, unsteadily and quite drunk, to kiss her, the city lights drifted like embers across the darkness. Her mouth was parted and warm; then she fled, the raindrops on her cape leaving a trail of trembling sparks. The next day she went away with her mother, a small gray wisp of a woman who never smiled, leaving him a note which read:

> My Dear Lieutenant Loftis,
> The dance was wonderful. I will be in Saratoga for a week. May I meet you in the lobby of the Ritz next Saturday afternoon? I think you understand.
> Helen

He was trapped, and he was married five months later on the island, with the bright hollow panoply attending such military affairs - the ceremony that disturbed him because of the untroubled thrill it gave him, not the mere sense of patriotic urgency, the spinal excitement that came from the flags and the music, but because of the more or less unwarranted pride he felt in his rank ( a captaincy now) which, in spite of the fact that it was secured only through his bride, and he knew it, made him nonetheless feel a fierce adolescent upsurge of exciting arrogance - the twin silver bars and the starched dress uniform, impeccably white - and the feeling of disquietude was not dispelled by the news brought by his father, now a diffidently mild, still doting old man in whom patience was no longer a virtue but a habit, who stood shyly in one corner of the officers' club at the reception, the ends of his once-proud moustache twitching sadly, and told him in an apologetic mournful tone that Charley Quinn had been killed overseas, and that it was bad, too bad, while the anger and outrage mounted silently in the younger man as he expressed a faint regret for the death of a boy he had lost track of long ago, barely concealing the resentment he felt at having been told such a thing on his wedding day, as if his father, in vague atonement for his own perhaps ill-advised move in procuring his son's commission in the first place, had passed the remark as a reminder that war was not all champagne and flowers and the gay brittle laughter of officers' wives. And he had hardly restrained himself from saying something bitter and insulting to the old man as he stood there, the damp feeble blinking of his eyes accentuating the weakness for which his son had felt all his life a quiet contempt, wanting to say _I know I know goddamit you think Im a slacker_, wanting to get him out of there and on his way back to Washington (_after all he was free now he had a wife he was free now hadn't five drunken years of college proved that Christ sake couldnt you ever get away from your father?_) - until a sudden, quick ache of pity and sadness came over him and he fumbled stupidly for a word to say _father, father_ and then Helen rustled up next to him, her face contorted with bliss, leading him away to meet someone, his father standing awkwardly in the corner now, groping in conversation with a bored young lieutenant while he (the new captain) listened to the rhythmic nuptial cliches of a general's wife, nodded, and thought of the pale boy with the blemish like a flower, the brother he never had, and of the father he had never found. "Really, Helen," the general's wife was saying, "I think you have the pick of the Army. Such a peach," and her laughter shattered the air like falling glass.

On the dock it was time for the train and the younger man, somberly eyeing the clock, leaned over and whispered in a tone of careful deference, "I think the train is late," while Ella Swan clucked forlornly, brushing the dust from her hands. "Lord Lord," she sighed. _Perhaps it isnt coming at all_, he thought, with the insistent unreason he had employed at other crises in his life which, out of the anxiety they entailed, demanded a momentary cessation of logic, he thinking now, _perhaps in all truth this is only a dream_, as when he had stood in a sweat of apprehension and horror in the offices of Dr Samuel Mordecai in Richmond while the doctor, a kindly Jew, lisping hesitantly, had told him that his daughter Maudie could never hope to progress beyond grammar school and that he must be brave about it, patient and tolerant, while he stood vertiginous and blinking incredulously in the newly-painted office smelling of turpentine, thinking _this surely isnt true, not me_, because he loved his daughter and even more - though he could scarcely admit it - he found the implications of the doctor's words almost too grotesque - _there had never been anyone in his family who was off in any way_ - "I know (the doctor talking now), but it does happen, you know. There are some things we can never understand," and he, as the doctor spoke, thought of the words, the hollow, devouring pity breathed with septic and pleasurable fascination over cocktails at the country club, "Isn't it a shame. She's retarded you know," but he left with the child, feeling for her more compassion than love, but loving her just the same, and determined that she would always have the best, the very best. So his second daughter, Peyton, whom he had wanted to be a boy, she - not his wife, nor Maudie - who received the extravagant outpouring of his love, was born a year later, a girl who although she did not become beautiful was not without beauty of a deeply speculative sort, possessing all her life - except the last year - a sullen and tenuous loveliness which transported a score of young men into witcheries of imponderable despair.

Perhaps it wont come at all

Ella Swan leaned out over the tracks and squinted into the sunlight, shielding her eyes with one hand. "Here come the train," she said. "Here she come. Lord have mercy!" Her whole body, as if stirred out of its calm and placid immobility by an electric shock, began to shudder, and she turned, saying, "Here come the train, Cap'n Loftis. What we goin' to do?"

"Take it easy, Ella," he said, "you'd better go over and sit down."

"No sir," she said, and her lips began to twitch gently. "I'm stayin' right here with you like I said. You need a woman right now even if she is a nigger and I'm stayin' right with you like I said."

"All right, but hush."

The engine eased slowly onto the dock and the three people stared up at the greased trembling wheels and were enveloped in in a vaporous plume of smoke. When the train came to a halt the younger man departed on noiseless feet in the direction of the baggage car, and the passengers stepped down, blinking up at the sun, and scuttled away with their bags into the station and out pf the drifting rain of dust. Milton Loftis saw Marcus Bonner, remembering with a thudding pain at his chest the distant voice the night before, metallic and remote above the wirehum of the telephone <u>Ive found her Captain Loftis</u>, <u>yes she is</u> <u>yes I dont know what to say</u> <u>yes sir</u> <u>yes Ill be with her</u> and the operator's fatuous automaton voice <u>Will you signal please</u> and the resonant humming silence Marcus pausing on the dock now as Loftis approached, brushing his sleeve, looking around for the person he expected to meet.

"Hello, Captain Loftis. It sure is dusty, isn't it?"

Loftis gestured toward the freighter. They walked together toward the street and stood waiting. Neither of them said a word as they watched them unload the steel case containing the body of Peyton Loftis from the baggage car onto the platform. Mr. Casper, the undertaker, supervised the operation, gesturing in a professional manner to the baggagemen, his mouse-gray gloves describing intricate arcs and circles in the air. Three little colored boys had gathered by the tracks to watch the procedure and Ella Swan shooed them away - "Git on outa here!" - and they fled in terror, trailing small excited squeals behind them. Marcus could hear a clattering noise on the freighter and a persistent, furious cry deep in the hold somewhere, "Come up there!" For a moment the case rested on a carriage near the hearse while Mr. Casper consulted with the baggagemen; for a few seconds it shone brightly in the sunlight and then, sifting down, the dust settled on the box and the glittering light faded.

Marcus and Milton Loftis walked over to the limousine, which was parked by the tracks near the hearse. As Mr. Casper and his assistant lifted the coffin into the hearse (in the tassled gloom the case looked too small for Peyton, even as Marcus remembered her) Ella Swan, bending into the doorway, whispered in a tiny, decrepit voice, "Peyton, honey, precious lamb."

Mr. Casper said, "We'd better go."

"Peyton, honey," Ella whimpered.

"Hush, Ella."

Mr. Casper led Ella to the car. She sat in the back with Marcus while Mr. Casper drove with Loftis beside him. They followed the dusty hearse down the waterfront, past the docks, and into town by a street lined with rustling elms.

## II

THE CAR proceeded into town, following the hearse which did not pause, Marcus noted, for the stoplights but eased past the intersections with a sleek and privileged gravity until, having crossed the overpass above the railroad, it came to Carver Avenue, newly named in recognition of the scientist at Tuskegee (an irony apparently lost upon the city fathers since previously the street had been known as Taliaferro - pronounced Tolliver - Avenue, after a minor statesman from the Piedmont who in the 'twenties courted a shortlived but nationwide fame as a violent advocate of states' rights and the polltax), a street improved now in name alone since despite the bright gleaming new street signs little else had changed since Marcus's last trip home: the avenue, the principal Negro street, was still lined on either side by the gray wooden two-storeyed shacks, the signs, scrawled in whitewash on the lower windows, advertising with vigorous and phonetic good cheer BarBQ and Restaraunt, the shacks themselves resisting decay and weather and even the cheap paint applied resolutely but without confidence once every ten years, defying age, rain, and the horror of the Northern tourists driving through, with the same indomitable resistance to the vagaries of the world that kept the owners of the shacks selling, year after year, BarBQ, Coke, and fried fish. This was the street that was made for Saturday night, for the rank smell of drugstore perfume, and the flick and rustle of smooth clinging silk on black bodies. They passed the Divine Joy Dance

Hall, a three storey frame building with peeling yellow paint and Marcus remembered - he hadn't thought of him for years - Clay, the boy who worked for Milton Loftis, standing by the porch, his black hand gripping the lawnmower handle, the lawn itself rich and sour with the odor of newmown grass, "Saturday night, Cap'n Loftis. Lord, listen. If you was a nigger on Taliaferro Avenue just one Saturday night you wouldn't want to be a white man no more."

In front, Milton Loftis's head nodded gently as the car bumped over a railroad spur. None of the four in the car had said a word since the train left the station. Marcus turned to Ella Swan: "How have you been, Ella?"

"Tol'able," she said, "I feered I ain't long for this here world."

"Nonsense. What's the matter? Your back?"

"Ain't my back." She took out a handkerchief and began to mop the dust off her face. "I got miseries all over. Seems like don't a day pass 'thout I got aches and pains."

"That's too bad."

"Ain't nothing but misery everywhere. We'll be saved, though, don't you worry, bless Jesus."

Marcus gazed out of the window.

"Peyton saved too, praise her heart."

"Shhh, Ella."

Milton Loftis turned around in his seat, looking at Ella and then at Marcus, regarding him for a moment with a helpless and imploring gaze, as if for an instant Ella's words had made him so conscious of his own shame and remorse that he could not utter a phrase of self-vindication, as if what the old woman had said -

"Peyton saved too" - had, in its tacit and unconscious blame, pinioned him helplessly in bands of inexpiable guilt, so that he could only stare into the eyes of someone he hoped would forgive him, gazing - his handsome flushed face twisted in pain - with the half-incredulous, stricken look of someone who has just killed someone he loves in a moment of rage.

As Loftis turned away Marcus was suddenly filled with an enormous contempt, and yet now - for the first time since he had learned about Loftis, had heard Peyton tell him one night in New York in a fury of grief and drunkenness the things he refused to believe until later when, carefully retrieving in his memory all those curious and unnamed gestures of the past, he came to know that the things she told him were true indeed - he felt for Loftis the first stirrings of, if not pity, then at least understanding, an understanding which was beginning to grow more even as he gazed silently at the flabby sunburned fold of skin at the back of Loftis's neck, a microscopically thin scurf of dandruff flaking the porous surface, knowing - or beginning to know - that what Sidney Harris had said was right when he told Marcus, *you can hate because hate is a physical thing, but you cannot take it upon yourself to condemn, ever*.

Near the end of the avenue the shacks and stores thinned out into a marshy, littered strip of land bordering a narrow creek. Two gastanks, rusty and enormous, rose out of the weeds and covered the road with their shadows. The air was full of the odor of coal gas and fish - a familiar, mingled smell. It reminded Marcus of Negroes. The hearse in front slowed down, the sudden slackening of speed and the final halt forcing the rear end into the air for an instant, as if ballooned up momentarily by gas, and then it settled down, trembling slightly, and the car came to an abrupt stop behind it.

"What is it?" Loftis looked out of the window. A barricade had been erected and a policeman was detouring traffic onto a side street.

Ella Swan leaned forward on the seat. "It's Daddy Faith," she whispered in awe.

Beyond the barricade a white-robed, turbaned throng was gathered around a glistening Cadillac convertible. Perched on the rich leather seat Daddy Faith was bestowing grace upon the crowd. He was smiling; his face, black as night, was greasy with sweat. He gestured with a glittering hand, his shiny opera hat and diamond stick-pin made beautiful flashes in the air. Behind the Cadillac somewhere a band was playing. A bass drum, in heavy counterpoint to the jubilant brass, made a deep thumping noise.

"Happy am I!" the crowd was singing.

"Happy am I!"

<u>Thump</u>

"Says my Redeemer!"

<u>Thump</u>

"Happy am I!"

"I am so happy!"

<u>Thump</u>

"Can't you get around those niggers?" Loftis said to Mr. Casper. "Tell that cop - " But already the policeman had motioned to the hearse to go on, and the car followed while Ella Swan peered out of the rear window at the receding Cadillac and said in a tone infinitely wistful as she raised her hand to wave, "Hey there Daddy."

Mr. Casper was a man of gentle perceptions and exquisite sensitivity. When, driving now along the street bordering the river, he noticed the strain that Milton Loftis was undergoing, the almost palpable tenseness which five years as a practicing mortician and ten years apprenticeship under his late father had taught him often precedes physical collapse, he stretched out a bony hand - sprinkled with pale brown freckles the size of dimes - and patted Loftis's knee.

"There, Cap'n," he murmured, "buck up."

Mr. Casper was a kindly man. Anguish communicated itself to him with the facility of a telegraph and his power as the extraordinarily acute receptor of mankind's most somber trouble had made him able, long ago, to distinguish between real and counterfeit grief. Consequently he felt Loftis's sorrow, and was keenly disturbed. He offered Loftis a cigarette, which was refused with a nod and a gently sibilant sigh-the tortured, pent-up breath escaping from parted lips - which Mr. Casper immediately recognized as that of a man who is on the verge of expressing his torment (generally in that incoherent sobbing convulsion which had always made him ill-at-ease), but who, usually through pride, restrains himself until the end. Whether the sufferer would finally give vent to his agony was always a matter of speculation for Mr. Casper, and one that kept him on edge - "tenterhooks" was the word he used in his infrequent discussions with his wife about business matters.

The situation had been made even more difficult today. He had received the Loftises' call the night before, not at home, but at the funeral parlor where he was going over his accounts with Mr. Huggins, the auditor for the Tidewater Morticians' Cooperative League. It was Mrs. Loftis's voice; he recognized it instantly (he had had a casual association with her from time to time in Community Chest work) - the cultured precise intonation, polite but faintly superior; she told him the facts, which he jotted down in a notebook, in a manner calm and devoid of feeling, and it was only after he had hung up, after murmuring the usual condolences, that he remarked to himself and then to Mr. Huggins, "that was funny, she sounded so . . . cold." And although his work had taught him that the profoundest feelings, for devious psychological reasons which he had no impulse to pursue, are often restrained beneath the most outwardly deceptive artifice, it was not without a sense of puzzlement, his professional inquisitiveness aroused, that he approached the Loftis house earlier that morning. He had no taste for the emotional congestion that usually afflicts women at such times of stress; often he had warned young Barclay, his assistant, that "a weeping woman is worse than a wildcat with wings," yielding to the young man one of his facetious epigrams, so carefully hoarded, that he believed tonic in relieving somewhat the austerity of their mission - like the cautionless, devil-may-care quip of a soldier before battle. But at the same time there stirred within him a wholesome solicitude, both personal and professional, which out of the very nature of his work demanded that the bereaved - especially a woman - manifest some small token of distress, if only pale, quivering lips trying bravely to smile; eyes which, though dry, expressed a depthless, ineffable grief. His heart was great, his very soul sought out the stricken and the lost - those whom he might for a moment console and encourage, those whose eyes, seeking solace, found his, tender and understanding, those upon whose burdened shoulders he might spread his own comforting balm of sympathy, before the last, the dust and the bitter earth, the return to an eternal rest.

That morning Helen Loftis greeted him at the door, her face as composed as if she were meeting the groceryman. True, he reflected, with a sudden stab of apprehension, her face was worn. A fine threadlike tapestry of wrinkles had traced itself across the ghostly face. A pity, he thought, a pity. But they - those tiny lines and convolutions, defining, like a chart, the story of suffering - had been there before. They, along with the lovely hair, stark white although she could not yet be fifty, belonged to another sorrow. Good heavens, he thought. She made an attempt to smile.

"Come in, Mr. Casper. Captain Loftis is upstairs. He'll be right down."

"Thank you, ma'am. I want to say - " The words of consolation began to rattle in his head like dominoes. "I want to say - "

"That's quite all right, Mr. Casper, won't you come in?"

He entered the screened-in porch hesitantly, unnerved and bewildered. The morning sun was hot against his back. Around the porch hovered the odor of azaleas, the murmurous sound of bees.

"I should like - " he began.

"Please, Mr. Casper," she said (a bit impatiently, he thought), "if you'll just sit here my husband will be down in a minute." She disappeared into the house, her silk wrapper making a wierd rustling noise behind her. He sank into the glider, warm with the smell of leather, and he began to sweat. Throught the windows he could see the diningroom, shadowy, empty. The crystal service, laid out in precision along the sideboard, reflected pools of light against the wall. Her work, he thought - ordered, neat, precise.

Milton Loftis came down. His eyes were bloodshot, and he spoke in a voice that was husky and tired. It was to be strictly private, there was to be no announcement in the newspapers; no, none at all. Everyone would know later, anyway. Flowers? No, they wouldn't be necessary. The funeral would be at the graveside. Yes, he knew it was out of the ordinary but the rector had given his sanction. Yes (with a thin unhappy smile), yes he was tired, thank you, he was at the end of his tether.

Loftis went into the hallway and Mr. Casper sat down again and felt the warm green leather beneath his perspiring hands. It was all so strange, he thought. Beyond the porch the pale-blue waveless surface of Hampton Roads rested in a sultry calm. Far out, on the Norfolk side, the tiny purple silhouette of a battleship floated like a toy boat on a bathtub lake. An insolent gull squawked over the beach, soared upward and out of sight. The water, slick with oil, lay in a drowsy, inviolate stillness.

Mr. Casper heard voices floating from the hallway, faint and disembodied. Uneasily he lit a cigarette. Loftis was saying, "And so you aren't coming with me," and she, "Why should I? I told you

I'd come by myself. Later." And,

He: Helen, haven't you even

She: Please. I told you. I don't want to say anything else about it.

Mr. Casper held his breath, so he could hear.

He: But just decency demands

She: Yes decency. Yes decency. Yes go on and talk about decency.

He (imploring): Helen dont you realize

She (bitterly): Yes yes. I realize everything. Everything.

He: But I cant go alone. You said You know yourself What will people

She (mockingly): Ha! What will people think! I know. What will people think! Dont make me laugh.

He ( in a tone of subdued entreaty ): Helen just listen to me please

She: Ill listen.

He: Weve been over everything. I cant say anymore. It seems that youd do just this one thing, not for me

She (sarcastically): But for Peyton.

He: Helen dont talk like that. You dont know what youre saying. You

She: Milton Im tired. Im going upstairs now.

He (flatly): So you arent coming, huh.

She: No (footsteps moving across the floor) Why dont you take Dolly

He (sorrowfully): Oh Helen Oh Helen dear

<u>She</u>: Why dont you

<u>He</u>: Helen for Christs sake dont say

<u>She</u>: Or take Ella. Take a nigger. <u>She</u> loved Peyton.

<u>Silence</u>. <u>And</u> <u>softly</u>,

You dont know what youre saying. You cant.

Oh yes (<u>mounting</u> <u>footsteps</u> <u>on</u> <u>the</u> <u>stairs</u>) I can.

Oh <u>yes</u> I can. I <u>can</u>.

now

Good heavens, Mr. Casper thought.

###

34

DETOUR
ROAD UNDER CONSTRUCTION

Another policeman, spraddle-legged, stood at a barricade, his face beef-red and impervious behind amber sunglasses. Black crescents of perspiration soaked the armpits of his skyblue shirt and he gestured langourously with a gloved hand. Once more the limousine swelled quietly to a halt behind the hearse and Marcus saw Loftis jerk his neck in a tense impatient motion.

"The road," Mr. Casper said, "the road is under construction."

"I can see that," Loftis snapped.

"Lawd, is we ever goin' to git there," Ella Swan said.

The hearse backed up, pressing close for a moment to the front of the limousine, and Marcus caught a glimpse of the coffin, pale and metallic in the cool shadows. Then the car followed the hearse down a street which led back into the other part of town, past the pseudo-Rhenish towers of the old brewery, long ago deserted, its brick spires and battlements having fallen into dusty and crumbling decay even long before the time when Marcus, as a child, knew it only as a place suggesting something faintly sinister and clandestine, where before Prohibition (the older folks had said) there always was a sweet and heady, vaguely sickening, smell of fermenting malt until (thank the dear Lord) the Volstead Act came in, putting an end to its evil and ruinous influence forever because when the Repeal was effected the brewery was not considered a profitable enough a venture to resume operating in that teetotaling part of the country, and so for years afterwards it remained on the bleak tract of land on the border of town, the honeysuckle and hollyhocks and Virginia creeper trailing gradually over the deserted brick parapets and a gray accretion of dust from the nearby coalyards smoking the windows until on fine Saturday afternoons amid the dank odor of hollyhocks and dandelions and the glow of sunlight on crumbling stone, small boys would shatter the black windows with rocks and holler fearfully through the echoing, deserted halls; past the green polluted stream that wound through a barren wasteland of bottles, rusted car-bodies, and garbage behind the gray unpainted shacks of the Negroes, about which Marcus as a child heard tales of delicious and outrageous horror concerning a huge Negro convict who, in a night of frenzied debauch celebrating his escape, fell into the stream and was drowned and who, since the body was never recovered, reappeared from the stream at night on each anniversary of his demise, covered with scum and foaming horribly at the mouth as he prowled the town in search of small boys to drag back to the unspeakable depths of his grave; past Newport Avenue, unpaved and muddy to this day, where the high-school boys would drive cars innocently borrowed from their fathers and ogle the Negro whores who leaned from faded balconies and shouted, "Gwan away fum here, white boys. Yawl too little."

Now they had passed the railroad tracks and, beyond the neat green lawns of the better residential section where grew spirea and boxwood and rosebushes, the river came into view once more, the water near the shore shimmering with windflaws, white with blossoming sails. The bridge, five miles long, cast a web of shadows on the waves and far out, beneath the draw uptilted like the leg of a dog, a tramp steamer made a smudge of smoke against the sky.

Ella wept softly. "Peyton, honey."

"Don't take on now," Marcus whispered. He grasped her arm gently; her voice trailed off into a small doleful hiccup, "Pre - cious lamb."

A stoplight at an intersection near the city limits caused the car to halt. The hearse ahead had gone through when the light was green, passed a truck lumbering along down the highway, and was out of sight.

"Barclay!" Mr. Casper hissed. "I told him to wait."

As they paused at the light Marcus smelled the odor of flowers and, turning, saw a beautiful young woman, trowel in hand, digging in a bed of dark brown earth while above her, in response to her small graceful motions, a rosebush trembled and swayed, dropping a shower of white petals like snow. On the

37

sunlit lawn an enormous white Persian cat dozed among wickets laid out for croquet, and the lovely crouching woman turned suddenly, staring at the car, and very slowly, in a gesture wonderfully delicate and feminine, raised her wrist to her brow. Marcus gazed at her and for a moment the car was full of the smell of roses and earth. Then the light changed and the car moved off and even when the woman was out of sight Marcus still saw the picture - suspended gracefully and immobile in time though now the woman had bent again toward her garden, the rosebush sending down its rain of petals once more, the cat stirring on the lawn - of the lovely tilted face and the small pale hand lifted over sweet, inquiring eyes, the picture itself as fragile as the sudden wakening memory, while drowsing off into sleep, of those ladies, seen on an old china plate, sitting idly beneath the willows, or of the house one lived in long ago. It brought back thoughts he had fought against for days (was it that the woman looked like her, he wondered, possessed some nameless quality of manner or bearing that made him so mindful of the dead girl ahead?). There were roses growing in the schoolyard; in the spring, although the teachers forbade it, the bushes were all plucked bare. On the playground the little girls turned their flower-faces skyward and laughed, and the blossoms, tucked into their hair, fell to the ground and were trampled amid the orange peels and crusts of sandwich bread. Peyton turned to Marcus and said contemptuously, "Little gentleman . . . little gentleman," and he turned away blushing, sick with remorse. It was May Day, the pageant was *Cinderella*, and because he was the smallest they made him the page boy. In his white costume he stood before the mirror and gazed, stricken, at his quivering puny legs and at the absurd red feather dangling before his eyes. The mirror reflected no manhood, his legs were like sandpipers', and he called out, "Aunt Edna! No!" But she shooed him away and at the pageant in an agony of shame he bent before Peyton with the silver slipper, she sniffing beneath her breath, "Little gentleman . . . skinny little gentleman."

He loved her. The day before, Marcus and Tommy Derwood had stood in the shadowed corridor of the school; about them hovered the odor of oil and dust. Tommy drew a picture on the wall and they sniggered together in imbecile childish lechery. "I would like to *do it* to Peyton Loftis," Marcus said, possessing not even a fragmentary idea of what *doing it* entailed, knowing only that to *do it* implied some mystical and probably very intricate act of communion between two people, an act in reality so divorced from the hazy concept of it in his mind that, to him, *doing it* might conceivably involve a football or a Monopoly set. But because Tommy Derwood was dirty, and treacherous, too, he told Elvina Kauffman, a rowdy, pie-faced girl who was Peyton's best friend, what Marcus had said, and Elvina told Peyton.

Peyton was lovely. She had dark red hair, not common

flaming red, but the color of brick at twilight. Her eyes were thoughtful and unhappy, and her laughter was always a laugh of derision - not unfriendly - but full of gentle scorn, because she was pretty and she knew it. She was eleven, and her voice had the sound of silver coins clinking together.

After May Day Miss Thomas took the class for a walk through the woods to study Nature. Along the river bank beds of ivy and honeysuckle crowded across the path, encroaching on fields parched brown with mown alfalfa. The boys' voices shrilled raucously in the quiet midday air; the girls, conversing in soft ladylike tones, sidled prissily around small damp places on the ground. Miss Thomas, her graceless legs clad in thick kneelength stockings, trudged at the head of the group, gesturing with an ancient walkingstick, and said, "Class, look now, a maple tree." In the sunny fields, moist with heat, there was a cricketing noonday sound: the locusts scraped incessantly in the glens. Marcus lagged behind alone. Ahead, a crowd of admirers paid court to Peyton's attentions, she chattering solemnly in her bright silver manner, and once as she looked back, regarding him with cool hostility, he thought he would pass away with shame. "I didn't mean to - " he said softly to himself, but the class had stopped for lunch, pausing in a shaded clearing where pineneedles rustled slickly underfoot. Later as he sat apart from the crowd, propped against a pine tree, eating a soggy peanut-butter sandwich, Elvina Kauffman leaped from behind a bush and clutched him by the arm.

Her breath was bad and a crust of ugly yellow matter clung around her nostrils. "Peyton says you're nasty," she said, smiling savagely, making him start with fear, "she used to love you but she hates you now because you're nasty." He tugged furiously away from her. "Little gentleman, little gentleman," she taunted. "Get away, get away," he shrieked, standing erect, "get away, you old . . . bitch." In the clearing the class stared at him in astonishment and as Peyton turned her eyes from him disdainfully, with an imperious toss of her lovely hair, Elvina, laughing, crawled back through the honeysuckle like a possum.

That afternoon in class he passed her a formal letter of apology, printed carefully on ruled notebook paper. Her reply, returned only after a long delay during which countless exquisite pangs of hope and despair had passed through him, read, in words of calamitous finality,

> Dear "Little Gentleman,"
> I do not want to continue our relation any farther.
> Happily yours,
> (Miss) Peyton Loftis

Elvina, sitting at the desk next to Peyton, nudged and smirked, waggled her tongue at him lewdly and, turning slowly, Peyton cocked one eyebrow, like a grownup woman, and gave him a cool, dissolving look of unpardoning and consummate scorn. She was a proud girl, and cruel, and Marcus felt the love and desolation wring his heart like hands.

White motes of chalkdust swirled in the slanting light of afternoon, thirty pencils scratched in the stillness. Marcus drowsed.

"Marcus Bonner!"

He snapped awake with a thump.

"Stand up!" Miss Thomas stood over him.

He trembled by his desk, flushed with confusion.

"Were you sleeping?"

"Yes'm, I guess."

"What do you mean, 'you guess'?" she said, scowling.

"I mean, yes'm, I was."

"Well then, sit down," she said, "and see if you can't stay awake."

"Yes'm," he sighed, sitting down, a hot humiliating sweat on his brow.

"Are you sick, boy?"

"No ma'am." The class shuffled noisily and giggled, eyeing him with pleasurable stares. <u>The capital of Brazil</u> . . . Marcus tried to concentrate but couldn't, and gazed out of the window where, hovering above the sill, a huge fly with an irridescent belly made a sluggish droning sound. Beyond, on the river, the sunlight smoldered, and still farther out, beneath the shadows of the other shore, bright vagrant embers sparkled on the waves. Close in along the bank a Negro fisherman in a seedy-looking catboat was evoking the wind, moaning, "Daaawn . . . daaawn," and near him a jumping mullet hopped

42

out of the water, splashing silver, and vanished. The sound he had been waiting for came: the shipyard whistle, swelling up out of the distance, two miles down the river, shattered the stillness: its tone was treble, musical, and very sad, rising now to its sonorous crescendo as the class scribbled away in the dusty room, gently piercing and sorrowful, reminding him - perhaps because it was music - of things past and passing, of the ways the sycamores cast trembling pools of light upon the ground, of the picture of his father, whom he had never met, standing on a pier in Holland long ago, wearing a derby and funny round collars, and beyond that the remembrance of things never seen at all, but only lost amid a sense of ancient and forgotten happenings, of the lovely dead ladies who danced in ancient cavernous halls to the tinkling noise of spinet music, and the sunny fields of Spain, dusty and silent at noon, and the way the morning light fell over the woods of England a thousand years ago, and beyond that - the sound of the whistle constant now, shrill and unceasing, the fly buzzing drowsily above the window sill - of things to come, of great deeds and fabled conquests, of Peyton - upon what strange shores would he love her? he wondered - who said mercilessly, "Lips that <u>swear</u> will never touch mine," he pursuing her, bold, muscular, black sinful tattoos wreathing arms and hairy chest until, crumpled and acquiescent, she yielded herself up, forgiving, into his enfolding arms - "Marcus, I love you!" - the wonderful whistle sound musical and familiar in the swarming dusty room, loud and unending, passing beyond the sphere of sound itself, and hearing.

#

44

## III

After Helen Loftis heard the limousine pull away from the curb, efortlessly and almost inaudibly, and down the asphalt drive, she stood in the upper hallway and examined her face in the mirror. A crone's face she thought, haggard and spooky. With pale translucent hands she swept back white tendrils of hair, pressing them against her head, pulling at the same time the skin of her face taut over frail cheekbones so that the web of lines and wrinkles, as if touched by some miraculous and restorative wand, vanished, and so that by squinting convergently into the glass and exercising a good deal of imagination a lovely metamorphosis took place: transfigured, she watched with narrowed eyes the smooth skin as glossy white as the petal of a gardenia, the round young lips, feeling a faint, if certain, sense of rejuvenation, a sudden glow of memory. Then she dropped her hands and saw the lines sink once more into her face like thin streams of water running over sand.

In her room, facing the water, everything was sunny and clean. A soft breeze, almost impalpable, shook the curtains ever so slightly and the holly leaves outside the window made a crisp rustling sound. On the sheets of her bed, still unmade, there was a damp place where she had been sleeping the night before. She picked up the morning newspaper. Another rift in Allied-Soviet relations was rumored in Trieste, a film actress, known for her legs, and an eminent bandleader with a face like a mouse were united, in their mutual vulgarity, in a ceremony yesterday at Las Vegas. Unable to concentrate, she put the paper down and walked to the window and then, as if in afterthought, turned slowly and picked up the paper again, rustling through it to the page of local news. There was no notice, she observed, of Peyton's death, not that it mattered to her, nor would it matter even if Milton - she seeing him for the first time in weeks last night - had not telephoned Frank Downs, his voice a mockery of ceremonial and tremulous grief as he whispered, "Yes, Frank, m'daughter, m'dear little girl is gone. I want you to be quiet for me, Frank. Yes, Frank, I know the word'll get around, but" - and sobbing into the mouthpiece then - "Frank boy, she's gone, she's gone from me!" - all this, she thought as she sat quietly listening, only to minimize his role in the crime, to try to keep inviolate in the midst of sin and grief and ~~desolation~~ disaster the vestiges of integrity which certainly not she alone knew he had already lost. "And so you'll keep it quiet, Frank. Not for me, but for her - " and more soberly now - "yes, under the most terrible circumstances . . . in New York . . ." moving his lips silently in answer to the voice on the phone, and then, "yes, Frank, I knew you would - " a final spasm working in his neck - "g'bye Frank," and returning slowly to his chair across from her, greedily swallowing the pale dregs of his sixth or seventh drink, pouring another straight and gazing, not at her, but with murky blue eyes at the floor.

He talked finally, reviewing, with slurred syllables and maudlin sentiment, places visited and old events, remembering Peyton, of whom, as he talked, occasionally weeping - one hand stretched fanwise before his eyes, his head cocked to the side while he sobbed with small choking sounds like a child - she herself could only recall the single insistent image of a girl, dressed in a hideous shade of green, who, no longer her daughter and no longer even her biological duplicate, having responded from childhood to the gradual but inflexible tropism exerted by her father until the marked facial resemblence itself, which everyone said that as a child she bore to her mother, disappeared, standing in the alcove on her wedding day - the last day, until this day of her burial, that she ever returned to Port Warwick - her eyes deeply shaded with mascara, her face taut and drawn with a kind of fierce, agonized, and hopeless rage, but lovely even then she, Helen, had to admit, lovely even beneath the pitiable and ruinous look of dissipation and despair which glowed in her sullen and

47

unhappy eyes, breathing fiercely, her mouth not two inches away, "And even on this day you're not satisfied unless you can make me unhappy. Mother! You call yourself mother. You're - you're" - her face twisted in a look of inarticulate scorn - "You're a devil!" the last word spat out with such intensity that even divested of other meaning it carried with it a sense of profound and unutterable loathing, while she stood there, regarding her mildly, having endured similar outbursts before, knowing beyond hope or even desire that they could never find each other again. "I could die the way you've treated Sidney. Because he's Jewish? Yes, because he's a Jew," and turning, tears in her eyes, and whispering, "The pride of the South. The pride of the South. God, how I hate you all," turning again, and glaring at her once more, "And you, you not even from the South. An Army brat. Jesus!" until she, Helen, had enough and said calmly, "When you're through, you and your husband may leave. Tell him goodbye for me. I'm not feeling well." and turned and left the alcove and went upstairs where Maudie lay face-down across her bed, clutching a bouquet of tiny pink roses and weeping because Peyton was so beautiful. Maudie . . .

"Why should she want to do it?" Milton said. "Why?"

She was very tired. She closed the paper and stretched out on the bed. A ribbon of sunlight fell across her breast. Long ago and long before Maudie died, he was tender, because we loved each other and we were both still young. He would leave in the morning for the office, kissing us both goodbye, and I would sit on the porch in the sunlight with Maudie in her carriage and watch the dayold snow and the streaks of ice like glass upon the asphalt road. We would take walks, Maudie and I, I pushing the carriage along the seawall, very slow and careful so as not to slip on the ice, watching Maudie first as she slept bundled up in the carriage and then the cold sand and the seashells below the seawall and the thick wavy crust of ice which rimmed the beach like salt and hearing the old-fashioned trolley which ran in those days rumble by us. There were cedars along the road then, heavy and bending with powdered snow, and we left the seawall and walked beneath them down the road. Where the Powers' place is now there used to be a little store where I'd buy groceries and I took Maudie out of the carriage and let her walk around a bit. How she got out of the store I don't know to this day, she was only two years old, but I turned from the clerk suddenly - a premonition perhaps it was - and I saw in that blinding patch of light Maudie stumbling through the snow toward the car-tracks, laughing, I could hear her, and the shadow of the trolley coming out of the cedars, the shadow more terrible even than the trolley itself, and a white dust of snow shaking from the cedar trees. "Maudie," I screamed, "Maudie," the sound of the scream like a pain in my ears, and I saw the trolley run over her and heard it come to a sudden rattling stop somewhere out of sight. I don't know how I got to her but I was bending over her, the motorman's face, flushed and full of terror, bending, too, his trembling mouth saying over and over again, "Oh my God, what did I do," as I watched the small crushed leg and Maudie's face cradled against the snow unbelievably red in an endless spasm of pain before she shrieked in unknowing agony and I felt the final stabbing horror and, fainting into the snow, felt even then my enormous and immeasurable guilt.

"And so Helen I appeal - I ap-peal only to your sense of duty as a mother. Not alone because of - of any sense of decency, but because a mother's love - "

For the first time she spoke. "I told you before. There's no more love left in me. It's all gone. It's all gone."

"All gone," he echoed, his eyes searching the walls.

She stood up suddenly and looked down at him. "I will not be seen with you again, anywhere."

"All gone," he repeated.

"I despize you," she said.

He rose from the chair unsteadily, approached her with outstretched arms. The ludicrous streak of silver hair lay aslant across his brow, and she turned away. "Honey," he said thickly, "oh, honey, let's be good to each other, just now. I mean just this once. Lemme stay here tonight."

"No," she said, "go back to Dolly."

For an instant he said nothing and then behind her he muttered, "It's my house," and for one moment, as if conjured out of time and remembrance by a note of music, those brief petulant words, as sullen as a child's, made her conscious of a sorrow and a desolation she had never in her life felt before. It was as if through those words alone she had divined the whole nature of this unhappy man, and of their life together: like the shrill whistle which sets an avalanche falling, the words let loose a flood of emotion within her, as wordless and profound as memory, and she felt closer to him for that moment than she had in years. Her eyes filled with tears and she blurted out, "Yes, stay, go on and stay if you want to!" rushing from the room and standing bewildered on the stairs, shouting back, "Stay if you want to! It's your house!" and running upstairs to her room, weeping helpless, unfamiliar tears.

She stirred drowsily, hot streams of sweat trailed down her cheek. The holly ~~leaves~~ tree scraped gently outside the window. *Mama, Mama, why does Peyton say that, Mama. Shhh, Maudie-Poo* . . .

She slept.

# TYPESCRIPT II

*Second Beginning (Fall 1948)*

Lie Down

My life hath known no father
Any road to any end may run

*Iphigenia in Tauris*

Riding down to Port Warwick from Richmond, the train begins to pick up speed on the outskirts of the city, past the tobacco factories with their ever-present haze of acrid, sweetish dust and past the rows of uniformly-brown clapboard houses which stretch down the hilly streets for miles, it seems, the hundreds of roof-tops all reflecting the pale light of dawn, past the suburban roads still sluggish and sleepy with early morning traffic, and rattling swiftly now over the long bridge which separates the last two hills where in the valley below you can see the James River winding beneath its acid-green, malignant crust of scum out past the chemical plants and more rows of clapboard houses and into the woods beyond. Suddenly the train is burrowing through the pine woods and the conductor, who looks middle-aged and respectable, like someone's favorite uncle, lurches through the car asking for tickets. If you are particularly alert at that unconscionable hour you notice his voice, which is somewhat guttural and negroid - certainly oddly fatuous-sounding after the accents of New York or Columbus or wherever you came from - and when you ask him how far it is to Port Warwick and he says, "ab<u>oot</u> eighty miles," you know you're in Tidewater Virginia. Then you settle back in your seat, your face feeling swollen and unwashed from the intermittent sleep you got sitting up the night before, and your gums sore from too many cigarettes, and you try to doze off, but the nap of the blue felt seat prickles your neck and so you sit up once more and cross your legs, gazing drowsily at the pipe manufacturer from Allentown P-A, next to you, who told you last night about his hobby, model trains, and the joke about the two college girls at the Hotel Astor, and whose sleek face, sprouting a faint gray crop of fine stubble, one day old, is now peacefully relaxed and immobile in sleep, his breath issuing from slightly parted lips in delicate sighs. Or, turning away, you look out at the pine woods sweeping past at sixty miles an hour, the trees standing close together, green and somnolent, and the brown-needled carpet of the forest floor dappled brightly in the early morning light until the white fog of smoke from the engine ahead swirls and dips against the window like a tattered scarf and obscures the view.

Now the sun is up and you see the mist lifting off the fields and in the middle of the fields the solitary cabins with their slim threads of smoke trailing out of plastered chimneys and the glow of a fire through an open door and at a crossing the sudden, swift tableau of a Negro and his hay-wagon and a lop-eared mule: the Negro with his mouth agape, exposing calcimine teeth, staring at the speeding train until the smoke obscures him, too, from view

3

and the one dark brown hand held cataleptic in the air. Stirring, the pipe manufacturer squints sleepyeyed out the window and grunts, "Where are we?" and you murmur, "Not far from Port Warwick, I hope," and as he turns on his side to sleep some more you finger your copy of the Richmond Times-Dispatch which the newsboy sold you an hour ago, and which you haven't read and won't read because maybe you have things on your mind; and instead you look out once more at the late summer landscape and the low sorrowful beauty of the tideland streams, turgid and involute and secret and winding through marshes full of small, darting, frightened noises and glistening and dead silent at noon except for a whistle, far off, and a distant rumble on the rails. And most likely, as the train streaks past the little log-road stations with names like Apex and Jewel, a couple of Negroes are working way out in the woods sawing timber and they hear the whistle of your train and one of them stands erect from his end of the saw, wiping away the beads of sweat gathered on his brow like tiny blisters, and says, "Man, dat choo-choo's goin' to Richmond," and the other says, "Naw, she goin' to Po't Wa'ick," and the first one says, happily, "Hoo-ee, dat's a poon-tang town, sho' enough," and they laugh, as the saw resumes its hot metallic rip and the sun burns down in the swarming, resonant silence.

Port Warwick is a shipbuilding city and the workers' houses begin where the marshlands end - the clean cheap clusters of plywood cottages springing out of the woods like toadstools - and now the men are going to work, their automobiles creeping southward along the highway past more groups of houses encroaching suddenly upon the desolation of the marshlands, the houses themselves backed up against the forest wall where, in their tiny backyards, the women are hanging clothes in the morning sunlight, turning pale white faces slowly toward the train going by. The train slows down and the pipe manufacturer awakes, perplexed and sleepy, and borrows your newspaper and drowsily studies the headlines and when you turn again the wilderness is gone, the suburban houses are rolling by, and the gray anonymous streets, and the supermarket signs. Then the town itself, which from the train looks like any other small city since one side of the track - in this case the Negro section - presents a less imposing view than the other side, which belongs to the white people; and then the freight yards - you are going slowly now beneath the overpasses - and finally the halt at the station dock which is the end of the line because beyond the dock and the station is the river which is five miles wide and a deep salty green.

You get up and say goodbye to the pipe manufacturer, who is going on across the bay by ferry, and you pull your bag from the rack and climb down off the train onto the station dock where the smell of the water is clean and refreshing after the flatulent warmth of the coach and where, thirty yards away, your girl or your friends are waiting with expectant grins. "Oh, there he is!" and as you walk toward them you've already forgotten the pipe manufacturer forever, and the ride down. It's going to be a hot day.

It was a weekday morning late in August nineteen-forty-six and the train was expected at nine-fourteen. At precisely nine o'clock a black shiny hearse, whose motor was so soundless that the effect was that of no motor at all, slid quietly to a stop on the station dock at Port Warwick, followed by an automobile commonly known as a "limousine" in the mortuary trade - a Packard, and also highly polished. The driver of the limousine, Mr. Llewellyn Casper, was the most prominent local undertaker, a slim, bespectacled man who wore gloves the color of house-mice, and whose face conveyed a look of sympathetic, thoughtful awareness. It was a homely, lightly freckled face, with the pale-blue abstracted eyes of most people who have flaming red hair such as his, and as he climbed solemnly from the front seat onto the dock and gently opened the rear door, he gave an impression of quiet, vigilant decorum, a man to whom one could certainly, on a day like this, entrust the cheerless details attendant upon the death of someone in the family.

As he opened the door and bent into the rear seat, he said, "We've got fifteen minutes, Captain Loftis. Do you want to wait in the station?"

From the back seat there emerged Milton Loftis, followed by Dolly Bonner and by an old Negro woman dressed in black silk and white lace collar and cuffs, as if for a funeral. Her name was Ella Swan.

"I think we'll wait on the dock, Mr. Casper," Loftis said.

"All right, sir, I'll be with you in a minute. Oh, Lyle!" He departed on sudden noiseless feet toward his assistant, Barclay, the hearse-driver, a pale young man in a black baggy suit who was bent over the hood of the hearse, peering at the faintly smoking engine. The other three walked slowly over to the shadows beneath the shed-like affair which covered the tracks, where another group of people had already gathered for the train. From somewhere beneath the dock steam was escaping: it made a shrill incessant whistle. Above the shed the sky was clear and cloudless and a deep violent blue, the sort of morning that promises heat and vague languid activity all day long. The air, already humid, partook of that fugitive quality peculiar to Southern waterfronts: a heavy brackish smell of creosote and tar and dead fish, with the sense in the background of something frying on a stove. Across from the dock, and separated from it by twenty yards or so of slick greasy water, a freighter lay tethered to its pier. Into the hold a gang of stevedores had begun to load a cargo of bauxite. From the pier there came a rattle and hum of an electric crane, a scorched galvanic smell of burnt metal. A workman's voice from the hold, hollow and sepulchral, like the echo from a cave, cried, "Bring her over!" and a dense fog of dust started to drift down from the ship, floating like smoke in an undulating, ruddy cloud which settled gently on the dock between the trainshed and began to tinge everything it touched with a fine, dusty sediment the color of rust. Most of the waiting people retreated into the station, pounding their clothes with their hands, but Loftis and the two women waited patiently beside the tracks while the haze settled down upon them soundlessly, seeping into their clothes and encrusting the wrinkled face of the old Negro in a dusty mask.

" . . . and she wouldn't come, she wouldn't come at all," Milton Loftis was saying. "I begged, I pleaded with her. 'Dear God,' I said, 'only decency demands that you come. This day of all days,' I said. 'Don't you understand,' I said. 'It's our daughter, our daughter, not just mine though Dear God,' I said, 'you've done your best to alienate and though I know I'm much to blame myself I hope you realize . . . "

"Po' ol' thing," Ella Swan murmured. She brushed gently at her sleeves, the dust rising in small billowing puffs.

It was 9:07. The flyspecked clock, reading Bulova, made a faintly audible whirr above them.

"I wish I could go see her," Dolly said softly. "I wish I could make her understand. Ah, it's all so sad . . . " She was a rather pretty woman in her early forties. She was dark and would perhaps have been beautiful except for a slightly receding chin which lent to her features an expression not so much of weakness as of fretfulness, as if at any moment her jaw and lips might tremble in sorrow, like a little girl's. She had been much publicized for her social activities and her picture, taken shortly after her wedding, had been printed in the local papers sometimes as often as twice a week for over a period of twenty years until until finally even she sensed the impropriety of the cloche hat and bangs which had given rise to idle and secret laughter about town. So she had had the picture replaced, somewhat regretfully, with another, newer one in which there no longer blossomed the youthful smile but which recorded with annoying permanence the small puffy folds beneath her eyes and the neck, flaccid and slightly wrinkled. She laid her hand lightly on Loftis's arm. "Milton, dear, do you think I should really be here? I want so to be with you, dearest. But Helen and all, and . . . "

"Hush," he said. "I've told you. We've got nothing to conceal. You've always been my dearest friend."

"Yes, Milton," she said compliantly. "I'm with you."

The hearse was parked near the coal elevator. Each time Mr. Casper bent over to explain to Barclay what was wrong with the motor, a gondola car was upturned on the tracks above them and his words were lost in the furious clattering roar of tons of coal plunging into a ship's hold.

"Lyle," he would begin, "perhaps the FAN BELT . . . ISN'T . . . TURNING OVER LYLE!" Nervously he wiped the dust from his cuffs. "Perhaps the fan belt isn't turning over." Barclay got into the front of the hearse, let the motor run for a few seconds, but the fan belt was working. He turned the motor off.

"Did you check . . . "

Reeeeeeep! CaaarWONG!

Mr. Casper felt a bitter exasperation tighten like a knot in his mind. He hadhad hardly any sleep the night before and the scene around him had a giddy and abstract air, like the time he had awakened from an ether dream. "Now Lyle," he said, "are you *sure* you checked the water?"

"Yes, sir," the boy said glumly.

"Because I warned you the last time. This hearse cost nearly five thousand dollars, son, and we don't want anything to happen to it, do we?"

Barclay looked up from the motor and Mr. Casper smiled down at him gently. He and Stella had no children of their own, and his relations with his young apprentices had always been warm and paternal.

Lyle was rather slow but in his silent, inoffensively sullen way he was a nice boy. Nice but . . . well, slow, and this was no day to fall down on the job. Mr. Casper felt the sudden weary pang of irritation return.

"Here boy, let me look in there," he said, removing his gloves.

He groped blindly forward, feeling a new spasm of annoyance each time his sleeve brushed against the engine. Suddenly, leaning over, he lost his balance and as he grabbed wildly for support his hand came in contact with a part of the radiator. A scalding pain ran the length of his arm.

"_Damnation_, Lyle!" He leaped away from the motor.

He clutched his hand in agony and looked down where a blister was already forming. It was only a small place, but it hurt, and the pain filled him with a quick irrational anger.

"Fix it, boy," he said, as softly as he could. "Fix that radiator. If you can't, I will."

Two Negro dockhands walked past, eyeing the scene in bewilderment. Mr. Casper heard a chuckle. "Dead wagon. Man!"

"Hurt bad, Mr. Casper?" Barclay said.

He felt ashamed at his ouburst. "No, wasn't anything." Above, the cars rocked and rumbled on the incline like toy trains at a carnival. A magnet as big as a giant's hand turned each upside down, and twenty tons of coal fell seaward.

_Reeeeeeep!_ _CaaarWONG!_

From somewhere beneath the trainshed the escaping steam made a shrill sibilant clamor; the dust sifted down, enveloped the dock in a drifting asthmatic fog, and down the tracks the two lone redcaps, hauling luggage from the station, darted and disappeared into the haze like phantoms. It was 9:12 - Loftis looked up at the clock, at the attenuated grimy finger of the minute hand which just then jerked ahead with a clicketing sound - and, glancing at Dolly, he started to say something. But his lips moved sundlessly and he turned away suddenly toward the river.

"What is it, dear?" Dolly said.

He said nothing, because he heard nothing, and because his mind at the moment was engrossed with the riddle of his own bewildering sorrow, a sorrow that confounded him not because he was unacquainted with disaster but because for the first time in his life he was unable to cut his trouble adrift, to shed it like some startling and unwelcome chrysalis and finally to explain it away as "one of those things," leaving him perhaps a bit regretful, but certainly unscarred. His face had become slack with grief; as he gazed at the water (through the dust the light on the waves had a bright opalescent quality, and the word "purity" came to his mind) his eyes wore an astonished expression, as if he were watching the scene for the first time. He was in his middle fifties and had been good-looking in his youth (one could see that), and although some of the old handsome traces remained, his face had fallen into a limp and negligent disrepair: a young man's face thickly distended into an unhealthy flabbiness, the skin over well-formed bones now porous and deeply flushed. Through his hair ran a wide streak of steel gray which had been there since adolescence and which, far from being disfiguring, had provided a flourish toward which strangers might direct admiring looks; about this streak of gray he had been quite vain and because of it he rarely wore a hat.

Ella Swan said, "Train gonna come soon. Peyton comin' on de nine fo'teen. Po' precious lamb." She began to sob quietly into an enormous lace handkerchief. She had a wrinkled, wizened face, like that of an aged monkey, and while she wept her eyes peeped damply up over the folds of the lace and darted all around the dock. "Bless her little ol' heart," she sniffled.

"Shh-sh-sh," said Dolly. She laid her hand on the old woman's arm. "_Shhh_ now, Ella. Don't."

As Loftis glanced at the clock - it was time now for the train - he felt a swift gnawing pain of anxiety. The desire to speak, to say anything at all, became unbearable. But, out of some compulsion which he couldn't explain even to himself, he remained silent. _I won't think too much about this I'll try to occupy my mind with the water instead._ On the ship across the way a brickred figure, trailing a cable, scurried along a catwalk, suddenly yelled into the hold, "Steady!" _Perhaps if I only think of this moment, this second, the train won't come at all Perhaps it's possible to make time stop by not acknowledging the future, by thinking only of the present_, realizing, as he thought these things, that he was too old and too weary now for paradoxes, that he couldn't circumvent immediacy one bit, that the train would come after all, bringing with it the final, positive proof of fate and circumstance - words which all his life he had passively denied, because he was an Episcopalian and inclined neither by upbringing nor by conscience to brood long over abstractions. The train would come after all, bearing with it the conclusive totality of all his errors, and yet all his love - because he loved his daughter more than anything - and the thought which suddenly struck him - that of meeting her this morning, invisible within a coffin - filled him with horror. The train is now on the outskirts of town and passing with a terrible rumbling noise over the last creek and the colored shacks on the banks. He felt faint and sick. Nausea clutched at his stomach. He had to speak.

"Ah my God," he said weakly.

Ella Swan turned her face toward him. She dabbed softly at her eyes, saying, "Don't you worry none, Cap'n Milton. Me and Miss Dolly take keer of things nice and easy." She began to weep again. "Lawd God bless us Jesus," she sobbed, "we got de misery of dis yere world."

"Shh-hh, Ella," Dolly whispered.

I do not propose to convince, his father had said (in the feeble light of a March afternoon thirty years ago, before the house was torn down, but not long before, when even the lightest footstep in the hallway or upon the stairs sent a plaintive wooden squeal through the joists and beams, a fatal and ominous reminder not only of the swiftly aging house but of the passing of a finer, more tranquil age) I do not propose to convince you merely through paternal advice which no doubt you in your willful notion of filial duty would abjure anyway I only trust you will heed the warning of one who has seen much water pass as it were beneath the bridge one to whom I must admit the temptations of the flesh have been potent and manifold and that you will perhaps in some measure renounce a way of life which in its most charitable concept even can lead only to grief and heartbreak and possibly complete ruination I am an old man now . . .

So his father had known or somehow realized that the specter of his youth would rise up eventually to betray him, even though he could not have foreseen the final and irrevocable calamity - the son standing on the station dock, middle-aged and flabby, - awaiting the symbol of his doom - any more than he could have foreseen that another and crueller war would level the earth or that, long after his death, the Democrats would take over unbelievably for sixteen years. The vision of his father, flickering like an apparition across his brain, made Loftis feel a vague, indefinable bitterness. A wave of self-pity swept over him. He had the impulse to weep, to sit down by the tracks and cry like a child, but he fought it away from his mind. GOD DAMN it, anyway. The enormity of his sorrow was too much to bear. He had been defrauded by his youth. By a life which had begun innocently enough fifty-four years ago in a cluttered museum of a house in Washington, D.C., where his first memory was that of a sunny room murmurous with the sad, hushed sounds of Sunday afternoon and a parade outside on the street with distant band music both bright and disconsolate and his mother's voice whispering, "It's President Cleveland going by, Milton dear. Listen, dear." The sunlight was seeping in through gently rustling blinds and somewhere, infinitely far above, it had seemed, there was his mother's vacant hovering face, unseen and finally unknown because she died before he could picture in his consciousness those features his father later said were refined and lovely. There were also walks with his father in Rock Creek park and the damp ferny smell of the woods and his best friend, a boy named Charley Quinn, who had pale cheeks with famished hollows and a birthmark on his forehead like a brown-petalled flower, and who was killed at the Somme. *My son* . . .

*Your first duty remember son is always to yourself* (he was a lawyer, descended from a long line of lawyers, and until his death in 1920 he sported stiff wing collars and a twitching Edwardian moustache) *I do not intend to presume upon your own good judgment a faculty which I believe you possess in abundance inherited not from me but from your sainted mother so as you go out into the world I can only admonish you with the words of the Scotchman videlicet keep your sporran fast and your kilt down and let the wind blow* . . .

But his father lacked the prescience to avoid pampering his son and to realize that sending him to the University of Virginia, unprepared and at the age of seventeen, would produce the results it did: at nineteen he was a campus character known as "Blow," a drunkard even by fraternity standards who drank not so much because he liked the taste of whiskey and its attendant effects of surpassing goodwill, but because, fatherless, he found the sudden freedom oppressive. He combined glibness with a natural curiosity and when in his twenty-third year he was graduated from the law school he was pleasantly surprised, upon reviewing his record, that he had performed so well, considering that he had spent a preposterous amount of time drunk and in the town whorehouse, run by an elegant mulatto named Carmen Metz. And when the war broke out he did not shirk duty exactly, but made gestures toward joining the Army which years later he had to confess to himself were trifling and excursive, and he was greatly relieved when his father procured for him, through government connections, a commission in the Army legal branch. He was at Governors' Island during the entire war. The discipline was lax, he was young and handsome, and spoke in partly acquired, drawling accents that the gay young daughters of the staff officers found appealing. So, by processes more simple than he had ever imagined, he was promptly made a first lieutenant and then a captain - emerging from the war with that rank (a title which he retained as a civilian) and with the colonel's daughter. They met at an officers' dance on the island. Her name was Helen Peyton. Her father was a West Pointer, from an old Virginia family. Wasn't it a coincidence, she asked Milton as they danced, that her grandfather should have gone to the University, too? Afterwards they walked along the seawall in a drizzling rain, and when he bent over, unsteadily and quite drunk, to kiss her, the city lights drifted like embers across the darkness. Then she fled, the raindrops on her cape leaving a trail of trembling sparks. The next day she went away with her mother, a small gray wisp of a woman who never smiled, leaving him a note:

> My Dear Lieut. Loftis:
> The dance was wonderful. I will be in Saratoga for a week. May I meet you next Saturday at noon in the lobby of the Ritz? I think you understand.
> Helen Peyton

Perhaps they were both too young to know better, but they were married a few months later on the island, with the bright hollow panoply attending such military affairs: the ceremony that disturbed him because of the untroubled thrill it gave him. It wasn't the mere patriotic urgency, the spinal excitement that came from the sabers and the music that made him feel faintly ashamed. It was rather the unwarranted pride he had in his rank, which was secured only through his bride, and he knew it, but which nonetheless sent through him a fierce adolescent upsurge of exciting arrogance - the twin silver bars and the starched dress uniform, impeccably white. Nor was the vague sense of sham and delusion cancelled by the news brought by his father, now a diffidently mild, still doting old man in whom patience was no longer a virtue but a habit, who stood shyly in one corner of the officers' club at the reception, the ends of his once-proud moustache twitching sadly, and told him in an apologetic mournful tone that Charley Quinn had been killed overseas, that it was bad, too bad, while the anger and outrage mounted silently in the younger man as he expressed a faint regret for the death of a boy he had lost track of long ago, barely concealing the resentment he felt at having been told such a thing on his wedding day, as if his father, in atonement for his ill-advised move in procuring his son's commission in the first place, had passed the remark as an unwitting, perhaps unconscious reminder that war was not all champagne and flowers and the gay brittle laughter of officers' wives. And he had hardly restrained himself from saying something bitter and insulting to his father as the old man stood there, the damp feeble blinking of his eyes reflecting the weakness for which Loftis had felt all his life a quiet contempt, wanting to get him out of there and on his way back to Washington. *My son* (he was living in a boarding-house in Georgetown then, the old house had been condemned, torn down, and a government building erected on the site, the steel-and-concrete walls impermeable to the ghosts of a quiet and departed tradition or even to the memory of six acient cedars which had cast down a tender, trembling light upon that vanished ground) *my son your mother was a joy and indeed a deliverance to me and I hope and pray if only out of honor due to the blessed memory of her who brought you into life that you will as the Preacher said live* joyfully with the wife whom thou lovest all the days of the life of thy vanity which he hath given thee all the days of thy vanity for that is thy portion in this life and in thy labor which thou takest under the sun   My son . . .   A sudden quick ache of pity and sadness came over him, he fumbled stupidly for a word to say (Father, father) but Helen rustled up next to him, her face contorted with bliss, leading him away to meet someone. His father stood awkwardly in the corner then, groping in conversation with a bored young lieutenant while he (the new captain) listened to the rhythmic nuptial clichés of a general's wife, nodded, and thought of the pale boy with the blemish like a flower, the brother he never had, and of his father, whom he had never known. "Really, Helen, I think you have the pick of the Army. Such a peach," the general's wife was saying, and her laughter shattered the air like falling glass.

My son, Oh my son

The rubber pipe leading from the radiator had broken loose from its connection and most of the water had drained away onto the ground. Barclay went to fetch a bucket of water from the service station across the way. Mr. Casper fastened the hood and stood erect, wiping the grease carefully from his hands on a thick grimy wad of cotton waste. Then as he stood there, adjusting his tie, watching the dust sift down (he'd have to tell Lyle to run a cloth over the hearse), he heard a faint whistle far up the tracks. He looked at his watch: 9:20. The train. Above, a coal-car began to slide down the incline of the elevator: a wild descending lisp and squeak of steel against steel. The noise ground unbearably against his nerves and as he walked toward the group on the dock he thought that the day wasn't going well at all. Bad enough to be summoned at one a.m. for a simple transport job calling for neither embalming nor extras and worse yet to have the day drawn-out, like this one would be, sweltering, and in the end unprofitable. A black porter, emerging from the baggage-room laden with suitcases, brushed against him. Behind the screen door swung to, went slit-slap. "'Scuse me." "'Sallright." As he climbed the steps onto the dock a clean cool gust of salt air struck his face. He breathed in deeply, suddenly hearing Loftis's distant husky voice, high-pitched now and agitated, rocking tremulously on the edge of that sad hysteria he knew so well.

"I can't go through'th it," Loftis was saying, loud enough for a plump man passing Mr. Casper to stop and look back with a questioning stare, "I tell you . . . than I can bear . . . WON'T!" Mr. Casper was a kindly man. Anguish communicated itself to him with the facility of a telegraph and his power as the extraordinarily acute receptor of mankind's most somber trouble had made him able, long ago, to distinguish between genuine and counterfeit grief. This was the real thing. Approaching the group he heard the voice distincttly, quieter now but more tense, and penetrated by a low whispering undertone which was at the same time hoarse and curiously disembodied and utterly subdued. "No I won't go up there and see it now. No, I don't want to see it. No I won't. I can't. I'll just go . . . "

"All right, dear, if you want to," Dolly said soothingly. "You just go on. We'll meet Marcus."

The train rumbled ponderously onto the dock and sent down a vaporous white plume of smoke which swarmed and swirled around them and vanished, the engine shuddering to a stop and resting, panting like an abrupt and enormous beast beside them as the sunlight glinted brightly on a dozen greased wheels.

"I'll just go and sit in the car. I don't want to see it," he said quietly.

"Dat's right, Cap'n Milton," Ella Swan said, "you jes' go on over and rest yo' self. Me and Mr. Casper take keer of things nice and easy."

"There, Cap'n," Mr. Casper said, placing a hand gently on Loftis's shoulder. "Don't worry. Just go over and sit in the limousine. Everything's in my hands."

Loftis turned toward him with a look of relief, almost of deliverance, in his eyes, a wildeyed, grateful look that suddenly stirred Mr. Casper to a warm feeling of compassion, and he repeated softly, "Yes sir, you go sit down if you want to. Everything's in my hands." And Loftis hurried off toward the car, murmuring, "Yes, yes, I'll just go sit in the car," as if Mr. Casper's words had settled the whole issue.

When he had gone, Dolly burst into tears. "Poor Peyton," she wept, "poor poor girl." Her grief had a faintly spurious ring. Of course, it was difficult to tell about women. They were apt to to be fluently emotional when the opportunity for sorrow presented itself. He expected them to weep, after all, and it was unkind to jump to conclusions. But what was her connection with Loftis anyway? Something, a remark or a word he had heard, clamored for attention in the back of his mind, but it was quickly lost. He had things to do. As he walked up the tracks, peering through the dust for the baggage car, a troublesome sense of uncertainty began to come over him. He had felt it somehow all morning, and for a restless hour the night before, in bed; but it was only just now - perhaps it was the look on Dolly Bonner's face - that the uneasy feeling he had had, actually began to assert itself. There was something suspicious about the whole matter - nothing you could pin down, nothing, of course, really wrong in, say, the legal sense - but the entire sequnce of events, beginning the night before when he had first taken on the job, made him feel vaguely as if he were party to an act that was unprincipled, and somehow shameful.

He took pride in his work, and the fact that Mr. and Mrs. Loftis had adopted such an insensitive - even un-Christian - attitude toward the remains, the remains of their own daughter, shocked him and, in some obscure and circuitous manner, seemed an affront not only to him personally, but to the profession. But there was money in it, however little, and he couldn't quite refuse to go. He had received the Loftis's call the night before, not at his house, but at the funeral home where he was going over his accounts with Mr. Huggins, the auditor for the Tidewater Mortician's Cooperative League. It was Mrs. Loftis's voice; he recognized it instantly, having had a casual association with her from time to time in Community Chest work: the cultured, precise intonation, polite but faintly superior. She told him the facts - which he jotted down in a notebook - in a manner calm and devoid of feeling, and it was only after he had hung up, after murmuring the usual condolences, that he remarked to himself and then to Mr. Huggins: "That was funny, she sounded so . . . cold." His work had taught him that the profoundest feelings, for devious psychological reasons which he had no impulse to pursue, are often hidden beneath the most outwardly deceptive artifice, but he approached the Loftis home this morning with genuine curiosity. He had no taste for the emotional congestion which seems to afflict women at times of great strain; often he had warned Barclay that "a weeping woman is worse than a wildcat with wings," yielding to the boy one of his facetious epigrams, so carefully hoarded, that he believed tonic in relieving somewhat the austerity of their mission, like the cautionless, rake-hell quip of a soldier before battle. But at the same time there stirred within him a wholesome solicitude which out of the very nature of his work demanded that the bereaved - especially a woman - manifest some small token of distress, if only pale drawn lips trying bravely to smile, eyes which, though dry, expressed depthless, ineffable grief. His heart was great, his very soul sought out the stricken and the lost - those whom he might for a moment console and encourage; those whose eyes, seeking solace, found his, tender and understanding; those upon whose burdened shoulders he might spread his own comforting balm of sympathy, before the last, the dust and the bitter earth, the return to an eternal rest.

That morning Helen Loftis greeted him at the door, her face as composed as if she were meeting the groceryman. True, he thought, with a sudden stab of apprehension, her face was worn. A fine threadlike tapestry of wrinkles had traced itself across the ghostly face. A pity, he thought, a pity. But they - those tiny lines and convolutions, defining, like a chart, the story of suffering,- had been there before. They, along with the lovely hair, stark white although she could not yet be fifty, belonged to some older sorrow. Good heavens, he thought. She made an attempt to smile.

"Come in, Mr. Casper. Captain Loftis is upstairs. He'll be right down."

"Thank you, ma'am. I want to say - " The words of consolation began to rattle in his head like dominoes. "I want to say - "

"That's quite all right, Mr. Casper. Won't you come in?"

He entered the screened-in porch hesitantly, unnerved and

bewildered. The morning sun was hot against his back. Around the porch hovered the odor of honeysuckle, the murmurous sound of bees.

"I should like - " he began.

"Please, Mr. Casper," she said (a bit impatiently, he thought ), "if you'll just sit here my husband will be down in a minute." She disappeared into the house, her silk wrapper making a wierd rustling noise behind her. He sank into the glider, warm with the smell, of leather, and he began to sweat. Through the windows he could see the dining-room, shadowy, empty. The crystal service, laid out in precision on the sideboard, reflected pools of light against the walls. Her work, he thought - ordered, neat, precise.

Loftis came down. His eyes were bloodshot and he spoke softly, in a husky, tired voice. It was to be strictly private, there was to be no announcement in the newspapers; no, none at all, everyone would know later anyway. Flowers? No, they wouldn't be necessary The funeral would be at the graveside. Yes, he knew it was out of the ordinary but the rector had given his sanction. Yes ( with a thin unhappy smile ), yes he was tired, thank you. Yes, he was at the end of his tether.

Loftis went into the hallway, and Mr. Casper sat down again and felt the warm green leather beneath his perspiring hands. It was all so strange, he thought. Beyond the porch the pale-blue waveless surface of the bay rested in a sultry calm. Far out, on the Norfolk side, the tiny purple silhouette of a battleship floated like a toy boat on a bathtub lake. An insolent gull squawked over the beach, soared upward and out of sight. The water, slick with oil, lay in a drowsy, inviolate stillness. Ella Swan darted out onto the porch. When she saw Mr. Casper she burst into tears, and fled back through the door, sobbing, "Lawd, Cap'n Milton, he's here!"

Mr. Casper heard voices floating from the hallway. Uneasily he lit a cigarette. Loftis was saying, "And so you aren't coming with me," and she, "I told you I'd come with Mr. Carr," and,

He: Helen, haven't you even . . .

She: Please, I told you. I don't want to say anything else about it.

Mr. Casper held his breath, so he could hear.

He: But just decency demands . . .

She (bitterly): Yes, decency. Yes, decency. Yes, go on and talk about decency.

He (imploring): Helen, don't you realize . . .

She: Yes, yes, I realize everything. Everything.

He: But I can't go alone . . . you know yourself . . . what will people think . . .

She (mockingly): Ha! What will people think! I know, what will people think! (contemptuously) Don't make me laugh.

He (in a tone of subdued entreaty): Helen, just listen to me, please.

She: I'll listen.

He: I know it's useless to suggest now that we reconcile these terrible things . . . Well it seems that you'd do this one thing not for me

She(sarcastically): But for Peyton.

He (softly): Yes, for Peyton. *Our* daughter

She: Milton, I'm tired. I'm going upstairs. I slept badly. I'm going upstairs now.

He (imploring again): Helen, *please*.

She: No (footsteps moving across the floor). Why don't you take Dolly?

He: Helen, *please.*

She: Ella will go. I'm sure she'd go with you. *She* loved Peyton.

He: *Please*, Helen, *please.*

She: No (mounting footsteps on the stairs).

He: Please

She: No (the sound of a door closing, above).

*Good Heavens*, Mr. Casper thought.

She stands by the window in her room facing the water. Everything is sunny and clean. A soft breeze shakes the curtains ever so slightly, almost imperceptibly, as with the touch of a feeble and unseen hand, and the holly leaves outside the window respond, too, with faint dry rustlings to that feverish, nerly quiescent air which has drifted from the water at this time on every insufferable morning that she can remember, but only for an hour or so, finally ceasing, abruptly, exhausted, no later ever than nine o'clock, leaving the house sapped of air, devitalized, and filled with stifling, flagrant heat, like that which escapes from an oven. Fifteen years ago they had planted trees, but the soil, so the young landscape architect they had down from Richmond said, was too sandy there for shade trees to grow tall enough to protect the house, so they had had to endure the summers, often half-regretting the fact that they had built so close to the water, but not really, for there had been compensations: a private beach - isolated from the handsome, neighboring homes - and a spacious view of the harbor.

Downstairs she hears the screen door slam to, then the noise of feet on the gravel walk. There is no sound of voices. The limousine pulls away from the curb, effortlessly and almost inaudibly, and down the asphalt driveway. Then the house is quiet, utterly still, seemingly immersed in a silence that is all but palpable, not an ominous quiet, but hot and brooding, and broken only by the loud chatter of a single locust in the garden: the chattering noise at first remote, threatening, then shrill and ascending, like something sliding up a wire, scraping outside the window with a clamor that is at once stacatto, outraged, and inane. Then the noise stops suddenly, and the abrupt brooding silence is like an echo, a sound in her ears.

On the sheets of her bed there is a damp place where she had been sleeping the night before. She thinks _How many times have I or Ella let the beds go unmade this late in the morning? Not many._ She sits down on the side of the bed and picks up the morning newspaper, the one which she, not Milton, for the first time she could remember, had retrieved from the front steps almost at dawn this morning, an act which was so out of keeping with the serene and orderly character of her life that she remarks now not the fact that she did such a curious thing, but the fact that in doing it she gave no special thought to this strange departure from habit, but had reflected only at the time (standing on the porch not three hours ago, peering through the chilly dawn light at the deserted street), thinking then, no longer with grief, but flatly, almost abstractedly: _I have brought two children into life and I was a mother for twenty-eight years and this is the first day that I have awakened knowing that I am a mother no longer and that I shall never be a mother again._ She begins to read the newspaper. Another rift in Allied-Soviet relations is rumored in Berlin. A picture below shows a film actress, known for her legs, and an eminent bandleader with a face like a mouse, who were united yesterday in a ceremony at Las Vegas, the two of them clutched together before an airplane ramp in an attitude of taut anticipation: the one face, that of the girl, who has been wed three times before, lovely and doomed, and that of the man, who has been married only twice, whimsical and rodent-like and harmless, the carefully nurtured scrap of moustache emphasizing the very impotence it had been obviously cultivated to deny; yet both of them, man and woman, on the surface of whatever possible torment, wearing a mask of vacant Western bliss with the doggedness that affirmed they would be smiling that relentless smile even in the midst of the first or perhaps next wild clasped consummation, upon children named Christopher, Stephen, and Sandra, forever and ever. *Married*, she thinks, *married*, and she begins to read further, but she is unable to concentrate, seized by the sense of emptiness that has become more frequent and familiar during the past year: an emptiness that is not anguish nor anxiety nor even futility, but an abrupt physical sense of languor and infirmity, as if everything vital had suddenly drained forth from fiber and flesh, leaving her as limp and as helpless as some pale jelly that floats in the sea. She lays the paper down. Slowly she rises and walks to the window, touching the sill for a moment with her fingertips. The locust is still. Beyond the garden, the trellis and the swollen blooms of honeysuckle, the wilted azaleas, she hears a car pass on the road. The sound approaches, fades, dies. She thinks *Life* *others.* She turns and stands by the dresser and examines her face in the mirror. An old woman's face, she thinks, haggard and spooky. She sweeps back her white hair, pressing it against her head with hands that are pale, almost translucent. Beneath the shiny skin of her hands the veins are tessellated, like a blue mosaic, like an intricate blue design captured beneath glass. Now (she has done this before) she pulls the skin of her face taut over the cheekbones, so that the web of lines and wrinkles vanishes as if it has been touched by some miraculous and restorative wand, and she squints convergently into the glass, watching the foolish and illusory and lovely metamorphosis which takes place: transfigured, she sees the smooth skin, as glossy white as the petal of a gardenia or a rose, the lips which are not forty-eight but are sixteen or twenty and as unblemished by any sorrow as those she held up to a similar mirror over thirty years ago and whispered "Dearest" to an invisible and quite imaginary lover. She drops her hands and turns away from the glass and, as if in afterthought, walks over to the bed and picks up the paper again, rustling through it to the page of local news. There is no notice of Peyton's death. She scans the page again, abstractedly and witout purpose, not out of any expectation - because she knows no notice will be there - but rather out of the same languor and emptiness which have cancelled all desire and all hope and even most thought save memory itself, now remembering Milton the night before - seeing him for the first time in weeks - telephoning Frank Downs, the local publisher, in a voice of ceremonial and tremulous grief as he whispered, "Yes, Frank, my daughter, m'little girl's gone . . . so if you'll keep it out of the ob-o-obituaries. Yes Frank, I know the word'll get around, but - " and sobbing into the mouthpiece - "Frankie, boy, she's gone from me, she's gone!" He had come earlier in the evening as she stood, after her solitary supper, in the hallway. She his car draw up, halt, and his footsteps on the walk, slow and hesitant. It was nearly dusk. There had been a thunder shower earlier, the garden was wet and drooping. As he approached, a noisy flock of sparrows swooped up from the lawn on a sudden blast of wind, disappearing into a boxwood hedge, swallowed up and invisible, still cheeping raucously as the hedge showered down a tiny storm of rain. He stood at the door for a moment, his face flushed, distraught, bewildered, saying nothing, then murmured, "Helen, Peyton's dead," and entered. She made no reply, the sudden shock striking somewhere inside her chest like an electric bolt, the shock flickering at the tips of her fingers and numbing her cheeks, but receding swiftly as she remembered, thought _so_ _so_ _well_, receding even as swiftly as that storm drifting faintly grumbling over the ocean now, the high-massed, unseen clouds reflecting into the garden a pink flushed half-light, swiftly fading. In the kitchen, amid the distant clumsy rattle of pots and pans, Ella Swan was humming a wordless tune, submissive and remote and full of ancient woe.

She could tell that he was already half-tight. They sat down across from each other, she on the sofa and he in his chair by the liquor cabinet which had not been opened since he left the house four months before. He drank straight shots of bourbon from a new pint bottle of Old Forester, pouring the whiskey with faintly trembling fingers into a dusty wine glass he had found in the cabinet. He began to speak rapidly, in an agitated, rising voice, as if he found himself tilting in argument with an opponent louder and more hysterical than himself, halting only to drink, his head thrown back in the abrupt, mechanical motion she was so acquainted with, then bobbing forward suddenly as if by springs, the flushed face ugly and distorted for a moment in a quick spasm of distaste as if even after all these years he was unable still to cope with the taste, the smell of the stuff which had been for so long his balm and salvation.

"It was something violent and awful, Marcus said. Something terrible!" He paused, his eyes incredulous, confounded, and bemused, not yet grieving but perplexed, wearing the irresolute, random look of a man who is still plotting a way out, an escape. "I don't know how. I don't know!" he said, his voice becoming louder, "If that goddamn Jew bastard husband had anything to do with it! If that . . ."

"Sh-h-h, Milton, not so loud," she said quietly, impassively. She spoke to him twice that evening. This was one, thinking, as she spoke, *the suffering hasn't come quite yet. Not yet. It will take awhile longer. He doesn't quite believe it, believing with that implacable and fallible certitude of selfish men that he will never come by misfortune. The suffering will come sudden, though, and soon.* The night came quickly, the descent of darkness was almost tropical. Suddenly it was dark outside, and she arose silently and turned on a lamp. In the garden a lone frog made a shrill piping sound. She sat back down on the sofa, her hands folded across her lap in an attitude passive and serene, calmly regarding the man who was no longer her husband and yet not a stranger, but something somewhere between the two, the man who was saying now, "Helen, I swear I don't know . . . Riding over here in the car I was wondering what I'd say to you. Wondering because God knows we've lost something, Wondering because thirty years ago God knows I didn't think all this would happen." He would halt, thrusting his head in his hands for a moment, as if in concentration. Then he would drink, greedily, snatching the wine glass from the table in an abrupt savage motion and draining it in a gulp, replacing it on the edge of the table, from which it once fell unbroken and almost noiseless to the carpet. He leaned over unsteadily and picked it up, saying, "I didn't think all this would happen." He paused. "You won't believe me, Helen . . . " Another pause. Not looking at him any more, she gazed out of the casement window at the lone mimosa tree, bedraggled and spectral in the darkness, dripping rain. "You won't believe me but the first thing I thought of was you. God knows and you know there wasn't any call for it but I thought of you. You think I'm not telling the truth, don't you? You think I'm saying that because . . . You think . . . " He began to sob. "Oh, God knows what you think." _The Grief is coming now_, she said to herself, _he is beginning to know what suffering is. Perhaps that is good in a way. Even he. Perhaps that is good in a way for a man to know finally what a woman knows almost from the day she is born._ His crying stopped as suddenly as it began. He was silent for a moment. She heard him fumbling on the table with the whiskey. Outside the mimosa seemed to come alive, the pink mossy blooms groped at the air like hands. Something trembled, shuddered, sighed, although it was only the early evening wind. She heard the the frog's throbbing voice, a latesummer sound of waning life: feeble and steadfast and unafraid.

"Why don't you say something? What's the matter? Why don't you say something?"

She could feel him bending forward in the chair - the voice coming as from a great distance, not threatful, only querulous and tired: "Answer me, Helen. What's the matter? Don't you feel anything? You haven't said a word. You haven't said a word all night." Again he ceased talking. Her eyes on the mimosa, she saw the glow from the kitchen and, faint among the distant pantry sounds, heard Ella Swan's tireless, patient lament. She said nothing, sensing his bending form in the chair, the voice pleading, "Helen, say something to me. Helen! Now. Say something, Helen!"

_Perhaps not yet suffering_, she thought, _perhaps not yet Grief. But quick. And soon._

. . . . .

She sinks down on the bed, on the damp place, and stretches out across the sheets. The sunlight in the room does not fade, does not falter, it gleams without shadow on the walls and ceiling. In a vase on her dresser four dahlias are withering. There are so many things . . . She had forgotten them. There are so many things . . . She shuts her eyes for a moment. _I must throw them out_, she thinks, _the dahlias, I must throw them out before I leave_, and in the darkness the fancied smell of old rancid water is sour and strong. Now she opens her eyes. By the dahlias the light falls upon the figurine dresser-lamps, upon those beribboned 18th-century lords and ladies suspended timeless and unaltered and unalterable in some grave and prissy minuet, the light and the heat and the silence in the house suddenly all becoming one, with form, it seems, and with substance, inert, unyielding, and profound. She closes her eyes again, thinking _I must somehow get that fan fixed_, and slowly thinking _of course I should pull down the blinds_. Thinking drowsily _Carey Carr is coming at eleven he said I must be ready_, not moving or stirring because of the weariness that has emptied her like a vessel. Now remote and apart from the silence in the house, she is aware of faint noises outside: half-heard and half-remembered the sounds flit like shapes through her mind, a gull's cry, a car on the road, water sucking at the shore. She drowses somewhere between sleep and waking, seeing the sparrows' wild fluttering swoop once more and the trembling drops of rain. "Helen, Peyton's dead," he murmured, and entered. Then he was saying in the rapt and stricken voice, "Oh she was too young. Too fine. How _could_ I have let her go!" Ella Swan had gone home - after Milton told her the news - amid lamentations and cries of "Lawd have mercy," and wails. He teetered back from the kitchen and slumped across from her. The bottle of whiskey was empty and, unable to find another, he rummaged about in cabinets and drawers, muttering to himself like some chronic and fretful old man in search of his pills, until he produced an old bottle of sweet vermouth from which he began to drink, steadily, intent. He was silent for a long time and then softly, without bewilderment or amazement or frenzy: "Hum'ly, Helen, with all humid-" she watched him patiently as he tried to form the words, his tongue clutched to the roof of his mouth like a leech - "wiz all humility I ask you to take me back. I been a awful stink-" he paused, tried to smile- " 'scuse me honey. I been an awful damn fool." His tone became beguiling, deprecatory. He flapped one arm into space, toward God, or an invisible witness, or nothing. "She doesn't mean anything to me. Honestly. She doesn't mean a thing. You think Dolly's been anything but a friend to me, a real good friend?" He leaned forward confidingly. "Lissen, honey, she and I've been wonnerful friends, 'atsall. I know it's hard f'you to believe it. But that's all. Real wonnerful friends." For a moment he seemed to have forgotten all about Peyton. His face was absorbed and reminiscent, as if amid all his dark and tangled desolation he were contemplating some lighter, happier place, more tranquil and reassuring. " 'Member, Helen, 'member those trips we used to take up to Connellsville. How you'd never taken a drink until then and Edward give- gave you some . . . " He pondered nervously, and ran his fingers across his forehead. "Somep'n. Wasn't whiskey. Brandy! 'At's what it was! Brandy's what it was and you got tight. 'Tiddly,' you called it. 'Tiddly . . . '" She could feel his gaze and heard his snicker, the voice warm and patronizing now, like that of an uncle with a bored child. "Yes, 'tiddly,' you called it. 'Member you now just as drunk as the Dutchess. There you were. 'Whoo! I'm a bit tiddly,' you hollered, stumbling all around the house." He was laughing in thick little chuckles, and when he stopped his voice expired in a faint wistful sigh, like wind through a shutter, "Aaah-hah, I can see you now. Yep. We had a lot of fun up there . . . " As he spoke she had a fleeting memory of her sister's home in the Pennsylvania mountains, placid and serene among oaktrees and easy mountain sunshine and the easier money of Mellons and Fricks, where they had visited every summer in the twenties, and the thirties, too - the good life, the happy life - a hundred years ago. The house rested on top of a forested hill. There was a marvelous view, mountains and huge mossy outcroppings of granite encircled the house; one felt quite hemmed in, but pleasantly so. The mornings were full of chill blue smoke and the house, in the limp and tasseled baroque of the period, was full of a chill blue elegance, rambling and spacious. There was a flagstoned porch or veranda overlooking the valley, from the depths of which, made faint by an intervening growth of trees, the sound of highway traffic ascended, the only reminder of another, less comfortable world.

"Oh they were the days. And remember when those hornets or bees or whatever they were chased Peyton out of the woods up there where that outdoor fireplace was and how excited she was, yelling for me I can hear her now, 'The bees, Daddy, big and yaller,' I can hear her now, 'The bees,' OH - " halting, his face slack and shocked and distressed, as if he had had his hand in fire, and had only then felt the pain. His lips trembled. *He is going to cry again*, she said to herself, *he is going to cry*

"Peyton."

*He is feeling it now. Ah, that sorrow hurries like the wind.*

"Peyton."

*He is going to cry again.*

He thrust his head forward into his hands. "M'little girl."

*Yes perhaps now. Perhaps now it will be upturned that chalice he has borne of whatever constant immeasurable selflove not mean yet not quite as strong as sin* . . .

"My baby, my little baby girl."

. . . *upturned in this moment of his affliction and dishonor and find only there never that pride he would cherish to his breast like a lover but only Grief*    *Only Grief*

"Peyton."

Peacefully she drowses. She is not asleep, nor is she quite awake. Sleep is like a light that trembles and fades: it swells then recedes like waves on a shore, the light seaglimmering and fathomless, glowing warm and tender and aching on lost drowned shoals of memory as *Daddy*  *Daddy*, the voice sounds again, *the bees*  *the bees* and she looks up from that cold mountain pool by the veranda where improbable tropical fish swim restlessly beneath dank green interlaced mountain ferns, looks up startled and frightened and then amused from her morning tea-tray at that tiny figure fleeing out of the distant woods like a nymph or dryad suspended mothlike and fluttering on the sunlit mossy bank and floating down the bright slope with abandoned birdshrill cries of fear and delight: "The bees, Daddy, the bees!" *Why, the dear*, she thought, *she wandered up there all by herself* and warm and shivery with motherlonging she rose, her arms outstretched - *why my dearest baby*- but Milton was running from his lawnchair, intercepting her, laughing, tossing Peyton high, high in the air as the small prim skirt blossomed like a gaudy flower in the sky.

"Well, Queen, what does your majesty report?" The voices

approached.

"Big bees, Daddy," The voice was small and excited and breathless. "Big and yaller."

"Bees, huh? Did they bite, huh? Did they bite?"

"Unh-nh, they just made noise."

"How did they - "

"They went like this, Daddy. Listen, Daddy."

He was talking to her now, striding up with Peyton enthroned in his arms. "Baby says she is Queen of the Bees. Completely enchanted. They wouldn't sting her."

"Listen, Daddy, they went like this. Listen. Daddy!" she cried, tugging at his ear, "listen, Daddy."

"I'm listening, sweet."

"Zzzzzzzzzzzzzz"

"Well, now."

"Zzzzzzzzzzzzzz"

She sat back down again. The coffee was suddenly without taste and for a moment she felt a helpless exasperation. Now Milton was buzzing and Peyton was buzzing and the sister and the brother-in-law and the morose German cook converged all at once upon the veranda with mild fond murmurings of admiration and approval.

"She went exploring, didn't she?" said Marion.

"Come here to me," Edward said, squatting down, and Peyton rushed toward her uncle, shrieking, "Unca Eddie, I was in the woods!" Then she heard herself speaking, without anger, calmly: "Come here, Peyton, let me brush you off. You know you shouldn't go up there by yourself. You'll get lost."

Reluctantly Peyton left Edward's arms, sulking toward her. "But, Mama."

"Come here, now."

"Go to Mama and let her fix your hair," Milton said, "then we'll go for a long walk with Uncle Eddie."

Peyton stood stiffly against her as she brushed and combed and groomed.

"It won't hurt for her to go up there, honey," Milton said, "there's a fence you know, and Edward . . . "

"I know - " she said, lightly, and without conviction. She felt foolish and a hot embarrassed flush rose to her cheeks. Curiously, she had the sense that they were all watching her, and with a small forced laugh she said, "Mama's darling got awfully dirty, didn't she?" Peyton began to struggle and squirm, reaching for Milton, "Daddy, let's go for a walk now. Now, Daddy. Let's go for a walk." She held her tightly for a moment, but relaxed her grip, and Peyton tugged away toward her father as Edward laughed, "There! I'd love to go for a walk with such a pretty little girl."

She turned back toward the table and with a quick involuntary motion which she hardly noticed, pulled her coat up around her shoulders. She felt chilled and abruptly, terribly empty. The voices faded up the hill behind her. The German woman hovered near with a broom, between hoarse German wheezes muttering, "Dot child is spoilt aready, Missus Helen, He spoil her somp'n awful. You should take care."

"Yes," she said.

"She grow up to be lot of trouble. Me, I got five what got der bottoms spanked every day yet."

"Yes."

"I got no trouble with dem neither."

"No."

"She's a nice girl, though. Pretty. You got a pretty daughter there, Missus Helen. Me, I love children."

She said nothing. The feeling she had - disappointment, jealousy, whatever it was - had passed. She drank the rest of her coffee. Suddenly she wished she were back in Virginia, but that feeling, too, slipped quickly away. How silly, she thought, how silly to imagine that for that moment I held her against me it was he she was yearning for. How silly. Oh, how utterly silly and absurd. Why, last night she crawled over against me on the bed and said, "Mama, do you love me?" And I said and she said. Oh, how silly of me, and selfish. Oh, really now, Helen. She remembered . . . Her sister was picking tulips in the garden. She got up and walked past her into the house, hurrying through the spacious elegant rooms with an anticipation that she did not and could not deny but, rather, exulted in, rushing up the muffled carpeted stairs in a wishful greedy suspense like a child at Christmas and then, halting, tiptoed onto the shadowed sunporch where Maudie, tiny and coral-pink, slept amid rattles and woolen dogs and familiar infantsmelling bedclothes. She bent over and picked her up gently. The baby, waking from strange darkness into unfathomable light, began to cry, then, trusting and hungry, became quiet, after a while, in her mother's arms. "There there, baby," Helen whispered, "mother's here.

There, Maudie-poo." <u>My youngest and dearest</u>. She sat down with the child and the warmth and contentment began to steal over her like a cloak. She felt peaceful and strong and young, as if she could go on being a mother forever. She was twenty-four.

• • • • •

She is nearly asleep. Faintly she senses cold streams of sweat on her cheek, the sound of the locust once more, alien, chattering, remote. A ribbon of sunlight falls across her breast, and she thinks, dreams that: <u>long ago</u> and long before Maudie died he was tender then, because they loved each other and they were both still young. He would leave in the morning for the office, kissing them both goodbye, and she would sit on the porch in the sunlight with Maudie in her carriage and watch the dayold snow and the streaks of ice like glass upon the asphalt road. They would take walks, she and Maudie, and she would push the carriage along the seawall, very slow and careful so as not to slip on the ice, watching Maudie first as she slept bundled up in the carriage and then the cold sand and the seashells below them and the wavy crust of ice which rimmed the bay like salt, and hearing the old-fashioned trolley which ran in those days rumble past. There were sycamores along the road, heavy and bending with powdered snow, and they left the seawall and walked beneath them down the road. Where the Powers' place is now there used to be a little store where she'd buy her groceries and she took Maudie out of the carriage and let her walk around a bit. Then she turned from the clerk suddenly - a premonition perhaps she had - and she saw Maudie stumbling through the snow toward the cartracks, the cartracks, laughing, she could hear her, and the shadow of the trolley comingfrom the sycamores, the shadow more terrible even than the trolley itself, and a white dust of snow shaking down from the sycamores. "Maudie," she screamed, "Maudie!" - the sound of the scream like a pain in her ears, and she saw the trolley run over her and heard it come to a sudden rattling stop somewhere out of sight. Then she was bending over her, the motorman's face, flushed and full of terror, bending too, the mouth saying as if it were not a man but only a mouth, saying, trembling, saying over and over again, Christ Jesus what have I done what have I done as she watched the small crushed arm and Maudie's face cradled against the snow unbelievably red in an endless spasm of pain before shrieking in unknowing agony and before she felt the final stabbing horror and, fainting into the snow, knew even than her enormous, her immeasurable guilt.

Milton arose from his chair across from her, weaving toward her with outstretched arms. He could hardly walk. The streak of silver lay aslant across his brow; tears ran down his face like streams of oil, like sweat. "Let's be good. Oh, honey, les be good t'each other. Jus' now. I mean jus' now. Lemme stay here tonight."

She did not answer as she left the room and began to climb the stairs. For an instant he said nothing and then behind her he muttered, "It's my house," and for a moment, as if conjured out of time and remembrance by a note of music, those brief petulant words, as sullen as a child's, made her conscious of a desolation that she had never in her life known before. It was almost as if through those words alone she had divined the nature of this unhappy man, and of their life together. Her eyes filled with tears, and she blurted out, "Yes, stay, go on and stay if you want to," rushing upstairs and standing, bewildered, on the landing, shouting hoarsely back, "Stay if you want to! It's your house!" and running upstairs to her room, weeping helpless, unfamiliar tears as the voice below cried: "Helen! Helen, honey! Helen! HELEN!"

. . . . .

She stirs drowsily, the holly leaves scrape gently outside the window.

_Mama Mama, why does Peyton say that, Mama?_
_Shhh-h, Maudie-poo_

She sleeps.

# TYPESCRIPT III

*Continuation of Second Beginning*

*(Spring 1949)*

1-44

Now from the back of the limousine as Loftis sat slack-limbed and sweating and trembling a bit in one corner of the seat, motion, form, color beyond the window suddenly all leaped into perspective with a startling urgency and he thought, absently and without concern, _I'll remember the way this is_: a man not given to caprice or foolishness or fancy, knowing it and proud of the fact, yet saying to himself: _I'll remember this, I'll always remember this_: the suave indecent cleanness of the automobile in which he sat and outside, through the open window, a woman's crazy hat dribbling pink cloth flowers fading into the dust, mottled sunburned arms warding off the dust like sleet or snow, and the woman's countryfied voice receding faintly, "My, my, ain't this a shame," the dust obscuring the sunlight so that everything - station, people, and all - was enveloped by a ghostly, almost primeval, shade - as in a painting by Turner: a semitransparent and coppery glow in which even moving objects seemed to remain suspended, motionless and insubstantial, like flies in amber.

Although it was still early morning there was music from a restaurant across the street. A guitar strummed. A plaintive juke-box voice, gentle and long-suffering, sang distantly,

> _You know that you are free to go dear_
> _Don't worry if I start to cry_

and at intervals behind him the coal cars descended the incline with a frantic shriek. _I will always remember how this felt_, he thought vaguely, "Ah Lord." Nausea tugged at his stomach again. His head ached dully from the whiskey the night before. He began to squirm on the seat, throwing one leg up on the folded-down miniature chair in front of him, and then the other. With his hands clasped across his stomach, he began to twiddle his thumbs. Then he began to hum in a small falsetto tenor the tune playing on the juke-box. The dust began to sift through the windows in a sunny red cloud. He sneezed once, twice, then a whole succession of sneezes that ended in a broken strangled gasp. He paused, mouth agape, waiting for the last spasm, but it didn't come. He blew his nose, then leaned over and rolled up both rear windows. The sudden lack of air made the car intolerably hot. With the same absorption he might have used in repairing a watch he rolled both windows down again, and slid back against the seat. Then through the window he saw Barclay pass by, carrying a bucket of water in the direction of the hearse parked just ahead. Loftis leaped out of the door and walked after him, panting a little as he strode through the dust, calling out, "Hey! Oh, son!" By the front of the hearse the boy paused and turned questioningly.

"Oh, son!"

"Yes sir?" Barclay said. He was a pale, slim lad of about nineteen. He had pimples and on his upper lip a fringe of timid pubescent hair and he stood gaping in wonderment as Loftis bore down upon him, breathing heavily.

"Ah - uh, well," Loftis said. "Is it - "

The boy said nothing. Although it was not his fault, he was afraid that somehow he would be held to blame for the broken radiator pipe. All morning he had worried: whether he would please or not, worrying about the fit of his brand-new black suit. He was conscientious and incorruptible and right-minded, a young man born to worry. Already the complexities of life, and of his calling, were oppressive and somehow unjust; he worried about them too. The morning had given him no end of trouble, he was sure Mr. Casper was going to fire him, and because he had worried about that he had scarcely let himself notice Milton Loftis, even though he knew that the man standing before him was the nearest kin to the body - or remains - he had driven all this way to fetch.

"Yes sir?" he repeated hesitantly.

There was a faint grin on Loftis's face. "Uh . . . having trouble with the engine?"

The boy managed to smile back uneasily. "Yeah . . . Yes sir. Yes sir. It's fixed now, though." He turned toward the engine and opened the hood. "The pipe here . . . " _Poor guy_, he thought, _I reckon he is grief-stricken_.

Loftis leaned over his shoulder. "You know, these Packard motors are funny," Barclay heard loftis say, "They're funny. I had a Packard once back in thirty-six. Now I like Packards - I've got an Olds now - I like Packards okay. But I'll swear I had the damndest time with my feed line. I guess I took that car down to Pritchard's five times before I got it straightened out."

"Yes sir," Barclay said. He was pouring water into the radiator, the can held high and his elbow almost in Loftis's face.

Npw an Olds I like because of hydramatic drive. Here, let me help you there . . . " He grasped the can end edged in front of the boy. "Taller than you," he said with a thin chuckle. The water began to slop over the engine and Barclay thought _hell, I reckon I got_ to go get some more. "Some people don't like hydramatic drive. I do. Pickup's slower and all that, but if you drive around town as much as I do it's a pretty good thing. I've had t^h^ree Olds and I wouldn't trade for another." He was talking loudly and rapidly, over his shoulder, over the commotion around them - the sound of voices in the dust astonished and excited like those of children caught in a sudden rainshower - over the slam of the coal-cars. "Charley Pritchard tried to sell me a Packard last week, said I wouldn't have to be on any list. I says, 'No, an Olds is still good enough for me'." He put the bucket down and glanced at his hands. "You got something I can wipe off on?"

Barclay handed him a rag, thinking _the poor guy_, watching the nervous hands trembling with a sort of palsied agitation, running through the wad of cloth over and over again as if it were not just oil he was trying to rub away but blood perhaps, or some indwelling, ineradicable stain of guilt. _The poor guy_, Barclay thought, _what would Mr. Casper say to make him feel better_? Loftis paused then, looked around tentatively, aimlessly, as if he considered walking off toward town. His expression was not one of grief or fear or anything. He just stood there, the rag clutched tightly in his hand, his face beaded with sweat but as bland and as composed as a deacon's. _I should say_, the boy was thinking, _I reckon I should say " I want to express my sincerest . . . "_ but Loftis's face was suddenly the color of chalk or powder, an incredible color of white that Barclay had heard about but didn't think possible even in a corpse, let alone alive: the face still bland and composed and expressionless, but as drained of color as if color had never existed there, and he watched in a sort of bewitchment as the dry bloodless lips parted and said: "I'm sick."

Loftis did not say anything more. He stood with one hand lightly, almost casually resting on the fender of the hearse, the other hand still clutching the rag, and then slowly and leisurely with all of the lazy methodical somnolence of a man walking in his sleep he let the rag drop from his hand and then drifted away through the dust. As he started off across the street his first thought was _I mustn't get sick here, I must get to a place where I can vomit_, fighting back the nausea which surged up from his belly in hot demanding waves, and then somehow walking across the street and through the near-deserted restaurant, past the juke-box now mute and gaudy with shifting kaleidoscopic light, red and blue and green, and into the filthy toilet in the rear where in spasms, bending over an unflushed bowl full of some anomalous foul-smelling sludge, he was sick. Then afterwards he went out and sat on a stool at the counter, where he could watch the limousine - still shaken and chilled and trembling but feeling better as the nausea settled and subsided, thinking _I've got to get hold of myself. I've got to be a man._ A taxi-driver who had been eating at the other end of the counter got up and paid and went out, saying "See you, Hazel" as the screen door banged, and walked past the fly-specked window toward the train, sucking on a toothpick with the easy shiftless look of all taxi-drivers south of the Potomac, strolled past with that imperturbable worryless languor as Loftis watched him finally disappear beyond the windowframe, into the dust. Then he turned apathetically and without thought on the metal stool and, looking around him, found the place empty except for Hazel.

"Hiya, what'll it be?" the woman said.

"Coffee."

"Say, you look real sick," she said. "You must of hung one on last night." She went back to the coffee urn. There was a familiar sour odor about the place, not reminiscent of anything clean or particularly unclean, only the smell of grease and of stagnant dishwater and of flabby uneatable bakeshop pastries that had been standing around too long; he gagged and thought he would be sick, and would have, had he not just finished being sick. He started to leave, rose half-way up from the stool, but the woman returned with the coffee, saying, "I seen you run back to the gentlemen's room just now. I figured you was probably sick." He began to drink the coffee.

"Say, you got the shakes. What you need is a BC or something." He said nothing, thinking _if I can last out this day I might be all right. It'll get well before you're married, time cures all, repudiates disaster, grief. Must. Even Helen . . ._ "I told Haywood - he's the driver just left - you looked kind of green. I don't drink myself although I've always said what's good for the gander is good for the goose to turn around an old parable and deerlord knows a woman is heavy-laden enough to want to get inebriated once in a while, in fact . . . " He was thinking _quiet just hush quiet_, knowing that at another time he would have replied amiably, would in fact himself have broached any subject of possible interest - the weather, prices, even the God of the Baptists - would have invoked topics verging on the wildest absurdity, even, not so much because he wanted to be liked by everyone (which was true) or because he wanted to feel accepted by a class of people with whom he naturally felt ill-at-ease (which was also true, and a matter of considerable self-searching, since he was a lawyer and he felt the need for The Common Touch), but mainly because he liked to talk, because he liked the round meaningful shapes of words, and because he was afraid of being alone. Now the woman appalled him and filled him with desperation, and he had a sudden fright because for a moment he didn't seem to understand a word she said. She seemed to be one with the anxiety and the dust and the nausea: a symbol disembodied and detached yet fearfully purposeful of all that can plague a man when he most needs restfulness and ease. She was a tall rawboned sallow blonde of about forty with random bulging eyes and pushed-in masculine features and she leaned slackly against the glassed-in case full of razor-blades and stale cigars, gazing out of the window while she talked steadily and stridently and without enthusiasm, as if she were often listened to but seldom heard and knew it, as if it did not matter that no one ever declared affirmation or denial or approval, either Loftis now or that echoing, unlistening choir of taxidrivers and trainmen and casual drunks who gave back each day what abstracted grunts they could afford between swallows of beer and bites of apple pie. "No, I got nothing against drinking personally and as I say I can't see why a woman shouldn't drink either, this being a free country and all, ah, it's just that it doesn't behoove me personally to drink as I have been told by my doctor that I have a nervous temper and it isn't likely that I and intoxicants would rightly get along, fit pals you might say, though in fact it is a known truth that doctors often prescribe intoxicants for certain nervous disorders, ah, my sister-in-law in Newark, New Jersey had a chronic condition of the uterus and had to have it taken out and was prescribed by her doctor to take a shot of whiskey each night before retiring. That's the sister of my <u>helpmate</u>, if I might use the expression -"

- she paused, her lips compressed in a look of derision and scorn - "you ain't seen him, I guess, since I rarerly if ever seen you in here before . . . the _ninny_," she sneered; "well, pore thing, burdened as she was her husband left her just as . . . " On and on. Loftis got up with the coffee and walked toward one of the booths that lined the far wall.

"That'll be five cents," the woman said.

He turned very slowly, balancing the cup on the saucer in one hand, and laid a nickel on the counter, then headed once more for a booth. He sat down in a seat nearest the window. He sipped at the coffee, watching the limousine, thinking, _how can a man feel so wretched_? and saw Dolly coming down the steps from the dock, holding the handrail, descending with a graceless hippy tentative tread as if she thought high heels and tight jersey skirt might threaten to catapult her sprawling into the street if she weren't careful, and then floating through the dust in a hasteful blur of color toward the spot where Barclay was dusting off the hearse. Loftis saw her speak and tap the boy on the shoulder as he stood bending over, and then saw the boy rise up abruptly as if he had been shocked, and gesture toward the restaurant with a sudden startled upraised arm. Then Dolly approached through the dust and entered the restaurant. The screen door banged behind her. He rose, then sat down again. She sat across from him, saying: "I just couldn't stand up there any longer knowing that you were by yourself . . . suffering."

He sighed, said nothing.

"I wanted to be with you."

"Yes," he said.

Hazel came up, leaned against the booth, and said, "What'll it be? Coffee?"

"I'll have some hot tea," Dolly said.

"I swear, we run out of tea last night," she said. "I phoned the man up at Upchurch's two hours ago and he said he'd bring some right along. We have a right smart call for ice team this time a year but that man's near about as worthless as my husband. Them two . . . "

"Coffe, then," Dolly said quietly.

"With or without cream?"

"No cream. Just sugar," Dolly said.

"Sugar's right there by you," she said. "Anything else? We got . . . "

"No, no, no, no," Loftis said softly. "Nothing. Nothing. Just bring the coffee."

Hazel went back to the counter, vacantly singing _You know that you are free to go, dear_

Dolly laid her hand on his, and in a willful irritated gesture he drew his hand away. Her solicitude, her damp constant look of concern had gotten on his nerves, and he wished he hadn't brought her with him, wished that an hour ago, during the terrible moment of lonesomeness that had come over him when Helen had walked upstairs, he hadn't thought frantically _yes, why don't I take Dolly, yes, by God, she'll know how I feel_. Because her presence now, rather than soothing him, made him feel even more acutely their mutual predicament and the whole intolerable situation. Her eyes glistened with pure rapt adoration. It was a look which, before, might have made him sense an upwelling of happiness and well-being, but which now . . . it was embarrassing, in a way repellent.

"Dear, you'll just have to be brave," she said.

"I was sick," he said.

"Oh my darling."

"I vomited. Bile came up. I'd go to bed. Any other day."

"Oh my poor darling."

Under different circumstances he would have devoured her sentiment, would have basked in that limpid atmosphere of devotion like a cat in the sun. In the past few years he had relied upon this brooding gaze of love and longing, perhaps unconsciously enough, as one among the assortment of props and crutches - along with all the liquor, and with Peyton - which supported him against the unthinkable notion that his life was not rich and purposeful and full of rewards. That face, that gaze, that loving glance, he had believed, were reward enough. He had never questioned her complaisance; her industrious will to please, the desire to accomodate herself to his every mood, had existed ever since she had fallen in love with him, and she had never wavered. She was submissive and she worshipped him, and it was for these reasons that he loved her. It had been that way from the beginning: he talked and she listened, rapt and bemused, while somehow through this curious interplay of self-esteem and self-effacement there ran an undercurrent of emotion they were both obliged to call love.

They had first met eight years ago, although perhaps "met" is not quite the proper word, since in a town the size of Port Warwick it was inevitable that they should have known each other by sight and by reputation.

As in other small industrial cities in America, Port Warwick possessed no proper "middle class," and in spite of the fact that its attitudes were predominately Southern there was no group of people which might have been termed the "aristocracy." It became a corporate community only at the turn of the century - when a multi-millionaire from California decided that the site of the town ( he owned the railroad which ran down from Richmond) would make a good place to build a shipyard. At the time there was not much more there than a collection of cowpaths and ramshackle piers and beach-huts inhabited by waifs and strays and beachcombers whose purpose there was never quite known, even to themselves, and who came from God knows where but were probably cast off from the dingy coastal steamers that refuelled infrequently at the lone skeleton of a coal-pier which was the only, and unprofitable, reason for the railroad's existence. There was a single saloon, too, at the time, where the railroad stands now, a dim place with no windows where whiskey was sold at five cents a drink or by the quart at a dollar-twenty-five. There was also a whorehouse, which was an unpainted shack wit two whores - an elderly Negress from the Barbadoes and a twenty year old white girl, a deaf-mute who, so the story goes, plied her numb and insentient trade for nearly two years until the one local agent of the law, himself bent on pleasure, found her one quiet afternoon in bed with her throat slit from ear to ear and a razor in her hand. Two grocery stores and an office for the coal pier and a Confederate sailors' cemetery, long forgotten and choked with unsightly vegetation: these and the mudflats were about all. So, unlike most Southern towns, there was no landed gentry to contend with when Progress got started. There were no pillared edifices surrounded by trembling magnolias where the natural and undisputed arbiters of conduct - people with names like Fitzhugh and Stuart and Marshall - might supervise the goings and comings of their inferiors, no frail little ladies in ruined lace fretting with arthritic thumbs over some gray tattered remnant of the charge at Shiloh or Manassas or Fredericksburg, no terrible and picturesque old men who were indulged in because their half-demented Sabbath afternoon cries of abomination and iniquity were somehow gently reminiscent of a day long ago when God still wore a white robe and you could leave church with the Power and the Glory abiding with you and ringing in your ears. All these never existed there. Port Warwick was the New South, and tradition belonged to another time and certainly to another place.

The multimillionaire came with steel and rivets and a small army of Negro laborers and built his shipyard at the mouth of the river. It was an enormous plant even at the beginning. He erected the building which fifty years later was to develop into the one of the largest machine shops in the country directly over the place where lay the dead Confederate seamen - unfortunates of a naval rivalry which proved finally and ultimately the expediency of steel for warships; although perhaps in response to nothing more than his own sentiment - because most Southerners had forgotten the graveyard by then - the multimillionaire placed a small brass plaque on the machine shop wall, reading <u>Hic jacet</u> . . . It was an irony that went unnoticed, a Yankee remembering the Confederate dead. And so for a while the plaque was nearly all there was to attest to whoever might care to know that the town - though otherwise rootless and traditionless and without past glory - shared with the rest of the state and with the South a small part of their common heritage, if it was only the resting place of a score or so of nameless sailors who had battled for a lost cause and who themselves finally became forgotten beyond forgottenness, for the plaque, having been shaken loose in time by the racketing noise of the machinery - having been unreadable anyway because of the soot and the grime - was taken down and for one reason or another never replaced. But no one noticed this. As the shipyard grew the town grew, and when the shipyard ceased growing the town, in turn, ceased to grow.

A horde of people had descended upon the town, Negroes from the cotton and peanut patches across the river, fishermen and oystermen from the inlets and shallows up the bay who spoke in the anachronous, negroid, almost Elizabethan tongue of that region which had been isolated and by-passed for centuries, whose feet, according to legend, were webbed like those of a duck, and whose red leathery juiceless faces seemed to be perpetually twisted into a wry, half-smiling grimace, as if they might still be confronting the assault of sun and storm and spray: they didn't know how to use a welding torch, but they allowed as how they could quickly learn. These came, and the farm-bred young bachelors from the Carolina hills, living in boarding houses run by women known as Miss Estelle or Miss Lois, and going to the B.Y.P.U. on Sunday nights where they met morally disposed young girls, to whom they were eventually married. Another group came, too: engineers and draughtsmen, young men from Michigan State and V.P.I. and M.I.T. and, because the town was growing, many storeowners and professional men - doctors and dentists and lawyers, men like Milton Loftis.

In the middle 'thirties when the country club, of which Loftis was a charter member, was built a few miles outside of town on a bluff overlooking the river, Port Warwick was a town of some forty thousand people. The boom was over. The shipyard had endured the first World War and a turbulent adolescence, even the depression, and was not only a local but a national institution. The Negroes, who composed nearly a third of the population, lived in the middle of town in a sprawling wasteland of rag-tag jerrybuilt houses and lopsided tenements centering upon Talliaferro - pronounced Tolliver - Avenue, a thoroughfare bordered by fishmarkets and restaurants and clothing stores operated by small baldheaded Jews. At the periphery of this section began the residences of the hillborn Carolina bachelors, now married and bred, the urbanized fishermen and farmers and their children, the carpenters and welders and small storekeepers who dwelt in simple clapboard houses on street after street lined with rustling elms. They were poor but not impoverished. They had large families, and some of them had Fords or Chevrolets in which they drove to the movies faithfully on Saturday night and just as faithfully to church on Sunday, believing in a God that was not only jealous and angry but inflexibly just, believing it not indisputably like their fathers, but believing it with a sad wistful acquiescence nonetheless, and with a hope perhaps unattained by their neighbors - the white collar executives, the doctors and lawyers - many of whom believed because they were Southerners - they were brought up that way - but most of whom, had they had time to believe, would have believed out of desperation and even then would have been the last generation to believe in any God at all.

These last - "middle class" by ordinary American standards - were the new, or rather original, aristocracy, and it was in this manner - in assuming a patrician status that was gratuitous and synthetic but unquestioned, in appropriating a way of life which was not their inheritance, but certainly no one else's - that they divested themselves, at least locally, of the "middle class" stamp, and became Southern gentlemen. They built nice modern houses near the water where there was air stirring and a view. The raised well-mannered children, sent them to church, either Episcopal or Presbyterian, and to dancing school, and made sure that the transition from the perambulator to the convertible was accomplished with ease and dispatch. The rallying point for them and their children was the country club, an imperious and costly establishment which was not ornate but, like the Colonial river homes after it took its design, stylized, complacent, and splendid. There was a swimming pool with sapphire waters near the eighteenth hole. On summer nights the grounds were incandescent with floodlights, pale ghostly moths darted in the grass and colored waiters hovered in the shadows as from any of a dozen scattered lawn tables one could hear the softly blurred, chilly laughter of exquisite young girls and the sound of distant, captivating music. It had been there, on just such a night in 1938, that Loftis and Dolly had met.

At the time it all happened, Dolly was well into her second marriage and was thirty-three years old. She had lived all her life in Port Warwick. Her father, a sluggish, humorless man, died suddenly of a heart attack while working as a welder in the shipyard. This was in 1919. He left her mother an angular frame house which he himself had built in 1905, a five thousand dollar insurance policy, and the care of his only daughter who was fourteen years old when he died and who, in his own words, was already "getting too Goddamn grownup." What he meant by this was that her devotion - enough even at the age of ten for two full-grown women - had confounded him and in some inexplicable way had often embarrassed him to the point of fury. He had loved her, but he had always been a peevish sort of man, the only man, indeed, who ever resented her overpowering affection.

At any rate, after the insurance money ran out, her mother was forced to go to work as a saleslady in a stationery store downtown. She was also compelled to take in boarders so that she might appropriate the money necessary to keep her daughter well dressed. For Dolly had already acquired a slightly bewildered, ingratiating charm, which was really a form of aggression disguised as cuteness, and had begun to mingle with the group of older teen-agers whose parents owned the nice homes on the water, was accepted by them, in fact, because she was pretty and gay and, in spite of her nondescript and faintly questionable background, could be depended upon by the boys to be a good sport..All this her mother discovered required clothes and more clothes, but like her daughter she was devoted and yielding, if anxious, and was eager to see that Dolly got the best in life. Then a curious thing happened. It was as if Dolly had suddenly said, "I'll forget that I ever intended to become something I'm not." For there was a new boarder in the house, a bachelor, a fleshy, asthmatic man of about forty with soft hands and spectacles and a look of vague alarm. His name was Albert Brokenborough. He said little. His goings and comings were mysterious enough to the boarders: What, they wondered, made a body so unsocial? But one night at dinner a week or so after he arrived he startled everyone by saying, right out of the clear air: "Perhaps you might care to know what my business in Port Warwick might be . . . " His mouth was slightly stained with grease. Slowly he tilted moist eyes skyward. "I am an organist, unactive at present, although I still play upon occasion to select church gatherings. At present, being indisposed due to a lung ailment I have sought out a town near the sea where I might be able to remedy the aforesaid ailment - the salt air, you know - so that maybe I can continue later my repertory at the organ." He lapsed into silence again, adding hopefully in the tired, hesitant voice which was almost like a woman's, "I am also a notary public. I have been commissioned in this state. If you need . . . " and looking around then, at Miss Applewhite, the aging secretary, and at the two young men who were pipefitters, he said, "No, no, I reckon not."

Strangely, Dolly became quite fond of Albert. It was September then, and she was eighteen. The boys and girls with whom she had partied and danced had gone off, most of them, to colleges or preparatory schools. She had not taken a job yet, even though they were available, but was content to stay at home and read magazines or go to the movies. She and Albert were the only ones in the house during the day, except for the part-time colored girl, and although at first she thought Albert terribly shy, and a bore, it finally developed that he had interesting things to tell her, about the farm where he had spent his life in the mountains of North Carolina, for instance, and the untimely death of his childhood sweetheart, and his mother who, when she passed away two years before, had almost caused him to perish himself, of grief. Dolly pitied him and the stories he told of his tragic life and of his sorrows filled her with tenderness. She began to call him Uncle Albert. He brought her candy and once, when she burst into tears because she lacked things that other girls had, he gave her a five dollar bill and patted her gently on the knee. "Ah, girl, ah, dear girl," he sighed, "life is a trap, I fear. So much sorrow. So much frustration. Ah me."

One day early in October, during a spell of sultry weather, they rode out to the beach together on the decrepit trolley which bounced through a stretch of sunny marshland smelling of salt and decay, taking with them their bathing suits and a picnic basket which the colored girl had prepared. At the beach Dolly helpfully clutched Uncle Albert's hand as he toiled up beside her over the dunes with hoarse asthmatic wheezes. They changed into their bathing suits behind separate hillocks of sand and then ventured into the water once, but found the bottom so full of oyster shells that they contented themselves with lying in the sun, side by side on a blanket. The beach was practically deserted. The water was a deep glassy green. White caps far out foamed and vanished, and above them seagulls wheeled and dipped and coasted downward without a sound. They ate their lunch, then Dolly lay back drowsily and listened to Uncle Albert talk about organ music, about his ailment, and about his childhood sweetheart, Margaret, who had been called away because, indeed, she had been too pure for this earth. Uncle Albert was fat, Dolly thought, and so old, but that didn't matter at all: he was intelligent and understanding, he needed love so. An hour passed in silence. Waves washed ceaselessly at the shore. The sun began to tingle at her legs, but she felt warm and sleepy and full of a strange longing. Uncle Albert stirred and suddenly, gently took her hand; she felt something - his elbow, she thought - pressing against her hip. She rose up with a start, not looking at him.

"We should go, I guess," she said, "Mama shouldn't know we've been here."

"Yes, yes, " he said. "Yes we'd better go," He paused. "She was much like you. The same eyes, the same way . . . "

"Who?" Dolly said.

"Margaret," he said.

"Oh." She turned away.

"Blessed girl, blessed girl," he whispered, although she was unable to tell whether he spoke of Margaret or herself.

She rose, confused and faintly excited, and changed into her clothes behind a dune. On the way back in the trolley, feeling the cool sweat of his palm as he held her hand, she listened as he told her of his mother's legacy to him. It was a secret, but it amounted to a little more than twenty thosand dollars.

"Oh, Uncle Albert," she said, "she must have been so dear to you. Poor man." The longing returned. She had the sudden lazy urge to stretch out all her limbs, but she only managed to tremble a bit against him.

Smiling faintly, he looked down at her. "She was dear to me," he murmured, "like you," as, gently and sleepily, she laid her head on his shoulder, hardly remembering when they got off the trolley and, as if in a trance, walked down the back alley together, his arm a round her waist now, past the lush tangled honeysuckle and monstrous blooms of hollyhock growing close against the kitchen door, and through the house then and upstairs to his room. There, standing close-twined, sweating and shuddering together in a bright slash of sunlight, they had kissed somehow, and he had muttered in that now surprising womanish voice:" I've never done this before. I've never done this. Before God. I swear it. You must help me!" as languidly, yet almost witless with fear at the feel of the damp fat flesh beneath her hands, she had whispered, "Oh, no, Uncle Albert. Oh, Albert honey. Neither have I."

They were married a month later. The union, however, did not last long. For one thing, Albert's legacy turned out to be considerably smaller than twenty thousand dollars; it was, in fact, less than a fourth of that sum. He had promised her, too, that he would buy a house "somewhere up on the river," but after six months passed, and then a year, she resigned herself to living with Albert, as she had since the wedding, in his room at the rear of the house overlooking the alleyway and a lone and drooping locust tree. Then he became ill. His asthma got worse and he was forced to stay in bed. The doctor came to see him day after day, and she had to go to work, as a clerk in the classified department of the local newspaper. The feeling of tenderness she had for him never faltered; her heart ached for him, he seemed so helpless, so pathetic. Yet in a way she was glad, at the end of a honeymoon which shamed and distressed her in memory long after, that he never slept with her again. He lay instead on a cot in a tiny room adjoining the hallway, and after working during the day she would spend each evening with him, reading to him from magazines or from Elbert Hubbard's Scrapbook, although at times when he could breathe more easily he talked to her about himself: how he thought of giving up the organ and of going back with her to the mountains in North Carolina, to farm or perhaps teach. He had led an unfortunate life, there had been so many responsibilities: he spoke of his mother often. Once, one night as Dolly gently propped his head up over the vapor lamp, he told her shyly and with obvious embarrassment, amid labored gasps, how he had slept in the same bed with his mother until he was past thirty, first as a little child, to protect her from the bears, and then during his adolescence - after his father died - to ward off and keep her secure against thieves, and finally for no reason at all: out of habit he had crept into bed with the old womah until the night she died.

"Ah, dear sweet girl," he breathed, "could we but know what gives us cause to have such pain. Could we but know."

Then, after nearly a year, Albert's heart gave away, and he was carried off - Dolly knew to heaven - without a murmur on a windless summer night, lying thin and wrinkled on his cot like a collapsed balloon, and Dolly, though she could not imagine it, mourned not so much for Albert as for herself, because she had no one now to love.

A paragraph or so on Dolly's second, more genteel marriage
Her developing sophistication, another paragraph: the "common" girl who makes good
Meets Loftis at dance for Peyton at country club
First glimpse of Peyton — already, mutual jealousy betw. P. + Dolly
Portrait of Peyton
Or am I too far gone? Would like to write a war novel: these people give me the creeps

# Description of the Documents

*Prospectus*

Ribbon typescript; typing on rectos only; corrections in black pencil.
Foliation: 1-5, typed numerals.
Paper: 215 x 278 mm, thickness .11 mm, wove, watermarked 'EDUCO BOND' within crest device.

*Typescript I*

In three sections; all three are ribbon typescript; typing on rectos only; corrections and cancellations in black pencil; one correction on 50 (leaves [ tree) in blue-black ink; [i] marked 'Hold' in black ball-point pen.
Foliation: [i-iv] [1] 2-33, 33-50 [=55 leaves, two foliated '33']; 2-33, 33 with typed numerals; 34-50 with numerals handwritten in black pencil.
Paper: [i-iv] [1]-12 is 215 x 278 mm, thickness .11 mm, wove, watermark identical to that for prospectus leaves above; 13-33, 33 is 213 x 276 mm, thickness .09 mm, wove, watermarked 'CAREW | Merit Bond | RAG CONTENT | U.S.A.'; 34-50 is 213 x 277 mm, thickness .10 mm, wove, watermarked 'CAREW | TREASURY BOND | RAG CONTENT | U.S.A.'

*Typescript II*

In two copies, ribbon and carbon, on identical paper; typing on rectos only; corrections in black pencil; [i] marked 'Lie Down' in black pencil; the ribbon copy is facsimiled in this volume.

Foliation: [i], [1] 2-43, typed numerals.
Paper: 215 x 278 mm, thickness .06 mm, wove, watermarked 'MILLERS FALLS | ONION SKIN | COTTON CONTENT'.

*Typescript III*

Ribbon typescript; typing on rectos only; corrections and notes in black pencil.
Foliation: [1] 2-7, 7-20 [=21 leaves, two foliated '7'], [1] marked '1=44' in black pencil.
Paper: 216 x 283 mm, thickness .08 mm, wove, watermarked 'MILLERS FALLS | EZERASE | COTTON CONTENT'.